DEDICATION

I would like to dedicate this book to my family for supporting me (especially my sister, Darlene, for her encouragement to publish this book) in all that I am trying to accomplish in my life and for appreciating the hard work I have put into writing my books!

ACKNOWLEDGEMENTS

I would like to thank my family and friends for their support as I continue to do what I love to do! Writing poetry and stories, both fiction and non-fiction, has been a passion of mine since I was a young child. This is my fourth self-published book, and it is quite different from the others I have written. I hope to continue to write many more books to entertain all of you in the future!

TABLE OF CONTENTS

□

ACROSS THE STREET

A story about a quiet, upscale neighborhood surrounded by secrets and lies

Jeanna M. Marescalchi

INTRODUCTION

Friends and enemies, spouses, and lovers, secrets and lies are what you will find as you read this book! Nothing is as it seems and there are many pieces to everyone's puzzle. Each chapter will keep you guessing what will come next. Enjoy this fictional story about a quiet, upscale neighborhood surrounded by secrets and lies!

INSIGHT

It is a moderately sized beige house with tan shutters and white trim. It has not been attended to in years. There is chipped paint along the eaves and a broken windowpane or two. I vaguely remember the elderly man who once lived there as I would only catch a glimpse of him while he went to retrieve his mail from his roadside mailbox, which was seldom. I believe the house has been vacant now for a couple of years. Overgrown shrubs dominate the front of the house, hiding a brick walkway covered with weeds. The front lawn is in dire need of mowing.

I have been anxiously waiting for someone to buy this property with hopes that they will fix the needed repairs and spruce up the place as it has become somewhat of an eye sore within the neighborhood. With today's current market values, it must be worth a good chunk of change regardless of the present condition. I, myself, considered for a moment, to buy the house as an investment property but after a long and argumentative conversation with my husband, who wanted nothing to do with that idea, it was clear to me that it was not going to happen.

I do not know what ever happened to the elderly homeowner, I wondered from time to time if he passed away or just moved on to a nursing home. As I said, I never really saw him much at all, and I never saw any cars other than his own in the driveway. I am not sure if he had any family, I do not even know if he had a wife or children. I am assuming he was all alone, and now that I am dwelling on this, I wish I had met him. He could have been a nice man who wanted neighbors to visit him.

As I mentioned, the house was a bit of an eyesore. The neighbors around do not like the fact that the house is as rundown and unkept as it is. However, it has never been condemned by the town so it must be habitable inside. I have not seen what it looks like inside, nor have I seen the backyard, which I am sure is even more overgrown than the front.

Other houses in the neighborhood, including mine, are all unique styles and sizes. Some are vinyl sided while others are clapboard. Some have a one car garage and others have two. All the homes are generously sized with large backyards and long walkways from the street to the front entrance.

The neighborhood itself consists of well to do families with both parents holding prominent careers. I am, however, one of the few who does not work which explains why I am also one of the few, if not the only one, who does not have a housekeeper. You will see luxury vehicles in most driveways, or minivans of the homes where multiple children live. Lawns are perfectly manicured, and you will always see landscaping trucks up and down the street.

The neighbors, on the other hand, can be quite different from one another. Most are friendly and personable, fun to be around especially during block parties and other gatherings, but a few can be very snobby and judgmental. Some like to create gossip around the neighborhood. Typical of most neighborhoods, I guess. I enjoy having morning coffee and evening cocktails, well, sometimes afternoon cocktails, with my closest neighbors. I tend to spend most of my time with those who have children around the same age as my own and my children spend time together with a few of their children as well.

My son, Andrew, is a junior at the local community
college. He chose not to attend college away as most of
the kids in the neighborhood chose to do. My husband
and I were fine with his decision, and it saved us from
having large college debt. My daughter, Jolene, is a
senior at the local high school, not at a private school
like most attend in the neighborhood. My husband, Jake,
is the owner of a high-end construction company which
primarily builds luxury homes and developments all over
the country though he does not have to travel for work
much since he has project supervisors to over-see the
construction progress. Hence the reason we were able to
move into our beautiful, large home in this prestigious, if
you will, neighborhood, which at times reminds me of
the television series,
'Desperate Housewives,' minus all the housewives. Oh,
and my name is Victoria. I do not like to be called 'Vicky'
but one of my neighbors, Ava, insists on calling me by
that name, and I know it is just to aggravate me. Ava is
one of the snobbier neighbors on the street but her
husband, Michael, when he is around as he travels quite
a bit, is a nice man. I have always wondered what he
was doing with her. My closest neighbor is Mia. We
connected soon after we moved in, which was about
eight years ago and her children, Mathew, and Katy,
have been close friends of my kids ever since. Our
relationship also blossomed so easily because as a
successful author, she works from home, so we spend a
lot of time together while the kids are at school and the
husbands are at work. Her husband, Doug, is an
architect so needless to say, Jake and he always talk
shop when they get together. Mathew is away at college,
but Andrew spends time with him when he comes home
for breaks and holidays. Jolene and Katy attend high
school together and they both play on the same soccer
team.

Mia and I do seem to have some good times mimicking certain neighbors, childish I know, but it is fun. At times, our other close neighbor, Julie, joins in with us but she prefers to stay out of it most of the time. There are a few other neighbors within our social circle worth mentioning; Andrea, Elizabeth, and Grace, who are all friendly and we get together with them and their husbands, Greg, Dave, and Tom as much as possible during the weekends.

Jake and I and our children have built a solid life here in this neighborhood and we are happy here. My house is more than large enough for the four of us and our little dog, Teddy, who I have not mentioned yet. He has been with us since we bought this house. Although, I am missing my built-in pool that Jake promised me when we first moved in, Mia and Doug have one, so my kids always end up there when it is a muggy day. As do I for 'wine time.'

As for the town, it is small with a quaint downtown area with many little shops, boutiques and small restaurants and bars. There is a neighborhood market close by I prefer to shop at rather than the large supermarket outside of town. As I stated, it is a small town, so rumors spread easily, and secrets are hard to keep quiet. Overall, it is a lovely place to live without all the hustle and bustle, traffic and noise that come with living in a big city.

I believe I have painted a good picture of what my neighborhood and town are like. Now I will tell you what can happen in a neighborhood and town like mine.

NEIGHBORHOOD WATCH

It was a beautiful summer morning, about eighty-five degrees. The sprinklers were on throughout the neighborhood lawns. Young children were seen running through them from house to house. The neighbors did not mind. Our mail carrier, his name is Bob, was delivering the mail. He knew most of the neighbors personally as it had been his route for many years. I was sitting out on my front porch having a cup of coffee, waiting for Mia to join me. Then, I noticed Bob putting mail into the mailbox across the street. It has been a couple of years since I had seen that. I thought to myself, the property must have been sold and we should be getting new neighbors soon. I did not bother to ask him for any information, I preferred to speculate on my own. Mia showed up with her coffee and we started talking about the house across the street.

Within minutes after our conversation began, a moving truck pulled into the driveway of the house across the street. Mia and I were gawking and being obvious about it. We saw a young man, well, he looked to be younger than us, get out of the van and go to the back to roll up the door. We could see that it was full of boxes which must have been belongings and we could also see how handsome this young man was. He was wearing a white tank top, a "wife beaters" t shirt as they were once called back in the day. He had curly, black hair and an athletic physique and was quite tanned. He for a moment caught us staring at him from the distance but we just snickered and looked away. Soon after that, a maroon-colored BMW, which I am quite sure was brand new, pulled in behind the van in the driveway. A gorgeous blonde-haired woman came out of the driver's side door wearing a metallic gold bikini top and a tropical wrap skirt. It was hard not to stare at her perfect little figure. She was stunning and looked as if she had just come back from a photo shoot for a resort brochure. The two of them then walked out toward the back of the house and did not return. Mia and I continued our conversation but now we had more to talk about.

A couple of hours had passed, and I realized I had better get in to do some laundry and housework before Jake came home. Mia, on the other hand, was just passing time until her housekeeper finished her chores. We said goodbye and knew we would meet for coffee again the next morning.

Later, as I was getting dinner ready, I noticed the man across the street walking up to check for mail. My kitchen is in the front of my house. The window above the sink faces the street so I have an unobstructed view of a few of the homes across the street from me. Other than custom valances, I do not have window treatments in my kitchen area. The man, whatever his name is, looked up and noticed me once again staring at him. I was a little embarrassed. All I could do was throw him a great big smile and a wave. He smiled back and gave me a thumbs up.

After dinner, Andrew and Jolene went their separate ways. I was cleaning up and Jake went to put the trash out. As I was washing the dishes, I saw Jake and the man from the across the street talking on the sidewalk on our side of the street, which would lead me to believe the man approached Jake. They were standing out there for a while then Jake came back into the house. "What took you so long?" I asked. Jake replied, "Oh, I just met our new neighbor, Jeff. He seems nice, a bit young but someone I think we will get along well with. "Hmm, I thought I saw a moving van in the driveway this morning." I am not sure why I responded that way. I guess I did not want my husband to know I was being nosey like some of our neighbors.

Anyway, it was getting late, and Jake tends to go up to bed earlier than I since he is the one who needs to get up and go to work so while he is upstairs sleeping, I usually like to read while sitting with Teddy in my three-season porch which separates our garage from the main house, a breezeway as you could call it and that, too, faces the front. Our neighborhood tends to be incredibly quiet at night, but you can hear crickets and dogs barking. Sometimes you can even hear conversations from next door neighbors if they have their windows opened.

As I was fully engaged in my book, a romance novel, naturally, I heard a noise coming from my trash bins out front. I assumed it was a raccoon, but I was not sure. Teddy wears a bark collar, which unbelievably, does work so he rarely barks at anything. Not much of a watch dog. I then decided to go and check it out for myself. I always feel safe in our neighborhood, and we do have a neighborhood watch program in place.

When I was outside, I noticed a person running into Mia's backyard. She lives two houses down from me. I ran into my house to call her. It took a few rings before she answered but she eventually did. She did not seem to be alarmed or worried even though Doug was away on business, but that was Mia. She was more independent and did spend a lot of nights without her husband home due to his demanding work schedule. She ended our phone call by reassuring me that if she sees or hears anything during the night, she will call the police. I was still feeling a little uneasy and decided it was time for Teddy and me to head upstairs for the night.

The next morning, I was waiting for Mia to arrive for coffee time. She was never late but this morning she was running a bit behind. She was quiet compared to usual and did not want to talk about the night before. I did not press the issue as I figured it was because she was exhausted staying up all night worrying about the person I saw running into her backyard and she would never tell me that. We are good friends, good neighbors rather, but we do not spend time together outside of our cul-de-sac, well, other than attending the girls' soccer games and the occasional yoga class in town. Our coffee time was cut short as Mia said she had an appointment she needed to get to.

Later that afternoon, I noticed Jeff, the man or should I say the boy next door, since Jake was quick to tell me he was much younger than us, come out of his backyard. He was carrying a large metal box, like a toolbox of some kind. He did not catch me watching him this time. He put the box in the back of the moving van which was now empty since all the boxes had already been removed and brought into the house. The BMW was not in the driveway at the time, in fact, I had not seen the car in the driveway since the morning before. And then, I thought to myself, what about his car? I am assuming he does not own a moving van. I was starting to get intrigued by all my own questions and assumptions, but now it was time for me to get back to my housework.

As I was preparing dinner because that is what I do
every day unless I am lucky enough to have Jake
surprise me and take me out for a nice dinner, I noticed
out my kitchen window, the BMW pulling into the
driveway across the street. "Oh, she's back," I said to
myself but then I saw a woman come out of the driver's
side though this time, she was a brunette. Attractive,
from what I could see. A bit shorter than the blonde but
nonetheless, a similar model like figure. She walked out
towards the back of the house, and I thought that was
strange because I have yet to see anyone go through
the front door of the house which I guess would make
sense since the bushes and shrubs were so overgrown
around the entrance and walkway. Now I began to
question if the BMW is his car and does he have a couple
of girlfriends and since I am hooked on romance novels,
I began concocting one of my own in my head at that
moment.

When Jake came home from work, I decided to press
him for some information about Jeff, since after all he
was the one who had spoken to him. "Hey honey, what
did the guy next door talk to you about last night?" I
asked in a curious manner. He replied, "Oh, you mean
Jeff?" "Yes," I responded. Jake continued, "Nothing
much, he said he was starting over and wanted to know
more about the neighborhood so I told him once he gets
settled in, we would have him over for a barbecue or
something like that." "Oh, okay," I said. Jake then
commented back with a question, "Is that alright?" I
answered, "Yes, it's fine." Good," Jake replied, "It would
be nice to get to know him before some of the neighbors
get their claws into him." I laughed a bit and then said
"Yes, it would!" Jake had no idea how interested I was to
know more about Jeff or how much I wanted to go
across the street to introduce myself, so I felt it best to
restrain myself from doing that for now. Besides, I knew
I could still speculate about Jeff with Mia the next
morning over coffee.

Well, the next morning, coffee time with Mia was not as
much fun as usual since Ava, the snobbiest neighbor of
them all as I mentioned, walked up to my front porch
just to say hello as she put it but I

knew she had an ulterior motive. "Good morning, ladies," she said to the two of us. I responded, "Oh, good morning to you as well Ava, it's great to see you." "To what do we owe the pleasure of this visit?" I asked. Meanwhile, Mia was cringing and not saying anything. She looked uncomfortable but we all tend to look or feel that way when Ava comes around. "Well," Ava replied, "I heard we have new neighbors, and I was wondering if you ladies have met them yet." I stated, "I'm not sure it is them; it might be just him." Then I went ahead to elaborate on that comment, "Jake has met him, his name is Jeff, but he made no mention to Jake of others." Then suddenly, walking up from his driveway and crossing the street toward us was Jeff. Ava was quick to comment, "Now, isn't he a sight for sore eyes." I agreed with her but not aloud. As he approached the three of us on my front porch, he said very politely, "Good morning, I thought I'd come over to introduce myself. I'm Jeff, Jeff Stevens." Naturally, Ava was the first to respond, "Well, hello Jeff, I'm Ava. I live in the great big gray house at the end of the cul-de-sac. It's the biggest house on the street." Jeff chuckled for a minute, "I'm sure it is." Ava continued talking. "This is Mia and Vicky." I rushed to say, "It's Victoria...I live here in this house." Jeff then replied, "Oh, then Jake must be your husband? I met him briefly the other night." "That's right," I said. Then Mia abruptly interrupted, "Excuse me but I must go home. I just remembered I need to remind Katy to do something." So, as she was walking away, I said, "Ok, we'll talk later." And she replied. "Yes, later." Ava, too, had to get back to her Nanny, which left just Jeff and I on the stairs of the front porch. I was sitting on the top step, he, on the bottom step. I then proceeded to start up a conversation by asking what he does for work. He answered vaguely "I own a business." Naturally, I would then ask what kind of business, but I did not and the more I did not know about him, the more I wanted to talk to him. There was not anything else said before his cell phone rang. "Excuse me, but I need to answer this." He then rushed across the street before I could even say the words, "talk again soon."

SOUNDS IN THE NIGHT

It was late at night, though I went up to bed earlier than usual. I was looking out one of my bedroom windows. Our bedroom is quite oversized and there are windows facing the front, side and back of the house. It was a beautiful night with a cooler than usual summer breeze, so I had a few of the windows opened. All was quiet, as it normally is in the neighborhood at night, so I went to get into bed. I am not sure how long it was before I heard a faint scream. I jumped out of bed to check on Andrew and Jolene, but both were sound asleep. I wanted to wake up Jake, but I knew he would only try to convince me that it was just an animal I heard and as far as Teddy goes, well, he is oblivious to any sounds in the night since he buries himself under the blankets to sleep. I concluded that is must have been an animal and I did not hear the screaming sound again.

The next couple of mornings, Mia did not show up for our coffee times. That was not unusual during the fall and winter months, which we really do not have much of, but during the summer it was. I tried calling her cell phone and landline numbers, as she and I still have actual telephones in our houses, but she did not answer either one. So, I finally decided to walk over to her house to check if everything was okay. I had not even made it halfway when I saw her walking towards me. "I am sorry, I have been so busy the last couple of mornings, I didn't have time to meet for coffee," she said as soon as we got closer. I noticed a large bruise on her arm around the elbow area, as she was wearing a short sleeve blouse. "Oh," I replied, "I understand, we all have things we need to get done," and I could not help but ask, "what happened to your elbow?" She stood there for a moment, hesitating before answering, "Oh, I was carrying up the laundry basket and tripped on my own foot. It was rather comical." "Oh," I said with a surprise like tone, "if I had a housekeeper like you do, I would not be carrying laundry baskets upstairs." as I laughed just a little. She then added, "Well, sometimes I don't mind helping, it gives me something to do."

For the rest of the day, I could not get my mind off Mia's bruise. Was I making a big deal out of nothing? She could have fell carrying up laundry or she and Doug could have had an argument, though, I was quite sure Doug was still away on business. Now, I felt just like Ava, always wanting to know the scoop. I told myself I needed to focus on something else.

Later that evening, Teddy and I were sitting in the breezeway when again, I saw a person running not into Mia's backyard this time but out of her backyard. I jumped up and went to call the police. We do not live in a gated community and most of the backyards on our side of the street abut wooded areas while the backyards of the houses across the street are parallel to a dead-end road. Our yard is fully fenced in, but Mia's is not.

I ran up to wake Jake, the kids were both sleeping. The police arrived shortly, and I went out to the front walkway to meet them. "Ma'am are you the one who called the police?" the police officer asked. "Yes," I replied, "I saw someone running from my neighbor's yard, and a few nights ago, I saw someone running into their yard." The police officer waited a minute, "So, did you contact the police a few nights ago?" I did not know what to say, "Um, no, I did not...but I did call my neighbor to let her know what I saw." "Okay then, I will take a walk around the neighborhood and be in contact with you if we see anything suspicious." As the officer was slowly walking away, I said, "Thank you, Officer," in a grateful voice.

As we were walking back into the house, Jake asked me, "Victoria, why didn't you tell me about the other night, when you saw someone running into Doug and Mia's yard?" I took a minute to answer, "Well, I didn't want to wake you and I spoke to Mia on the phone right after." I was not going to continue but I needed to, "and Jake, last night, I heard what I thought was a scream in the middle of the night." He responded by saying exactly what I knew he would say, "It was probably an animal."

SECRETS AND LIES

The afternoon following the night I saw the person running from Mia's yard, Mia came knocking on my door which was a few hours later than I expected since most of the neighbors saw all the commotion the night before. "Why didn't you call me last night before calling the cops?" she asked in a snippy tone which was unlike her. "I just wanted all of us to feel safe." I did not know how else to answer her question. I then decided to just ask her right out, "Hey, Mia, is everything alright?" She took a moment before replying, "Yes, everything is fine?" Then she turned to walk away and as she was leaving, she turned back to look at me and said, "Thank you for your concern but it is not necessary." That is the moment I realized something was not right.
A couple of days passed, and it was later in the afternoon. Andrea and Grace came over unexpectedly, which was a pleasant surprise, since I had not seen them in a while, and I was more than ready to share a bottle of wine. They were both concerned about Mia, but I did not feel it was appropriate to talk about her at that time. We did, however, discuss the incidents with the person I saw and the new neighbor. They did not stay long, just for one glass of wine since it was close to dinner time and Jake had come home a little earlier from work.

During dinner, Andrew and Jolene had questions about what had happened a few nights before. Jake and I did not want them to worry so we downplayed the whole thing. After the kids were finished with their dinner, which is always before Jake and me, they went out to do whatever it is they do with their friends. This always allows Jake and I to have adult conversation time, if you will, before he goes off to bed early. He began to talk about Jeff. "Hey, I was thinking we should have a barbecue this weekend and invite Jeff from across the street." He continued, "since you haven't met him yet." And that is when I remembered I did not tell Jake about Jeff stopping by the other day and at that point, I felt a little funny telling him. I was not trying to hide it from him, it just did not come up in recent conversations. He was waiting for my response, "Oh, isn't that a little short notice, maybe he has plans already," I said. "Well, it won't hurt to ask," he replied. I then responded with a bit of hesitation, "Well, then I guess I could run across the street sometime tomorrow and invite him." Jake then said, "I'll invite him, since I
have already talked to him, no sense having you go over and introduce yourself. If he agrees to come to our barbecue, you'll meet him then." I was creating a bigger lie by the minute! I was thinking about coming clean with Jake at that moment but then I thought...I did not know what I thought. So, I did not say anything.

The following morning, I had errands to run so I did not meet up with Mia to have coffee. I was at the neighborhood market, and I noticed a maroon BMW in the parking lot. It looked exactly like the one I saw in Jeff's driveway. Ironically, as I was walking into the store, walking out of the store was the blonde woman I saw across the street that day. I gave her a little smile and then said a quick hello. She smiled and said hello back but then I decided to approach her. "Excuse me," I said very nicely. She replied "Yes, can I help you?" "You look familiar to me," I said, then quickly asked, "You don't happen to live at 5 Loftin Lane, do you?" She took a minute, "uh, no, I do not, but my brother does." "Oh, then I must have seen you there, I live across the street." I did not know why I told her that. "Well, "she said, "I am running late for an appointment." And that is when I knew she did not want to stay and chat with me. "Okay, maybe I will see you again sometime," that is all I could think to say to end our short conversation.
When I returned home from doing my errands, I noticed the moving truck was no longer across the street. There were no cars in the driveway but there was a motorcycle which I assumed was Jeff's. I

figured I better go over there and invite him to our barbecue then I could get the so-called introductions out of the way. As I was making my way over, I saw Mia coming out of Jeff's backyard. To say the least, I was extremely surprised! She did not see me at first, but I did continue walking across the street and ended up meeting her at the beginning of Jeff's driveway. I could not help but ask, "Mia, what are you doing here?" She looked to be a little frazzled. "Uh, um, uh...I just stopped by to ask if Jeff had a hammer I could borrow." I was even more confused, "Doug doesn't have a hammer?" I asked. Mia responded, "Oh, I'm sure he does, I just couldn't find it but he's in a business meeting and I did not want to bother him." She continued, "I needed a hammer to hang some pictures and you weren't home." At this point, I knew something was up since she did not have a hammer in her hands. Then Mia asked me, "What brings you over here?" I quickly answered, "Oh, Jake wanted me to invite him to a barbecue at our house this weekend." Mia seemed a little frustrated when I said that. "Well, I need to get home" she said in a rushing manner. "Okay," I said, "I guess I will see you soon." And away she went. Jeff then came walking up. "Hey, Victoria," he said in a pleasant voice. I was glad he did not call me Vicky. "Hi Jeff," I said in an even more pleasant voice. "My husband Jake wanted to, well, as did I also, well," I was stumbling with my words, "we wanted to invite you to our house this weekend for a little barbecue. Nothing big, just some grilled food and cold beer, do you drink beer?" I continued to babble, "the weather is looking quite nice for Saturday afternoon, if you are not busy." He replied rather quickly, "Sure, that sounds great!" "What can I bring, perhaps a bottle of wine for you?" I laughed, "Oh, you already know me I guess...we'll see you around 4 on Saturday." After confirming the plans, I went back across the street.

I was still curious as to why Mia was there. Why she had not asked another neighbor for a hammer. It did not really make sense to me. I could have been reading too much into it, but it gave me something to dwell on for the next couple of hours.

That evening, Jake and I were having a glass of wine, which does not usually happen much on a worknight for him. I mentioned to him that I did go across the street to invite Jeff over for the barbecue. He was excited that his plan was a go. Now, I just had to wait the next few days until we get together.

FRIENDS & ENEMIES

It was finally Saturday! I was excited to have Jeff over
tonight. At least now I have something to talk about, his
sister. During the day, Jake and I were setting up the
backyard and firepit. The kids had other plans with their
friends so, it was just going to be me, Jake, and Jeff. An
interesting evening ahead for sure. But then Mia stopped
by and invited herself over. What was I going to say? It
would have been odd for me to say no so, now it was
going to be the four of us as Doug was still away on
business.
It was just about 4 o'clock and we were ready for our
barbecue. Right on time, the doorbell rang. I opened the
door, and it was Jeff with Mia right behind him. He had a
bottle of wine with him, and she had a tray of decorated
cupcakes. "Come on in," I said, "Jake is in the back, Mia,
you can show Jeff how to get there, can't you?" I just
wanted them both outside so I could down a quick glass
of wine before the festivities began.
Things were comfortable, dinner was going great. We
had some laughs and Jake and Jeff talked shop for quite
a while but then the mood changed. Mia went in to use
our bathroom and Jeff followed. They were gone for a
bit, so I told Jake I had to grab something from the
kitchen, when I just wanted to check up on the two of
them.

When I entered the kitchen, I saw Jeff holding onto Mia's arm, and from where I was standing, it looked as if he was grasping onto it tightly. "Um, is everything okay?" I asked, concerned. Jeff quickly answered, "Yes, everything is fine. I'm going back out now." After Jeff left the kitchen, I naturally asked Mia, "What is going on Mia?" She hesitated a bit, "Nothing, I don't want to talk about it." "There is definitely something going on, it's obvious to me," I continued to say, "you need to tell me." She got a little teary eyed and replied, "I can't talk about it right now, not here, but we will talk about it tomorrow," she added, "I promise." Mia left after our vague conversation, but Jeff was still in the backyard with Jake. A few minutes later, I went back out and sat next to Jake near the fire. It was just small talk for the rest of the evening, but I could not help but stare at Jeff occasionally while wondering what happened between him and Mia earlier. The evening ended, and we said our goodnights.

The next morning, it was pouring out and we had some strong thunderstorms come through. I was eager to talk with Mia, so I called her cell phone, but she did not answer, then I called her landline and her daughter answered. She said she had just got in from a friend's house but her mom was not home so I thought she must have gone to the store or something.

A couple of hours passed, and the rain had stopped. Mia's kids, Mathew, who had just returned home from college that morning, and Katy, came to our door looking for their mother. They said she had not come home yet, and her phone was on the kitchen counter. I was getting worried, so I yelled for Jake. He came running, "What's wrong, Victoria?" I responded with a concerned voice, "Mia is not at home, she's missing!" Jake had the kids come into the house and he called the police. I had a bad feeling...something did not seem right. I knew deep down that something bad must have happened to Mia. Andrew walked in and asked what was going on. I told him we were waiting for the police to arrive because

Mia was missing. He and Mathew went out to search around the neighborhood for her. Jolene and Katy went to a few of the neighbors' houses to ask if any of them had seen Mia within the past few hours.

When the police arrived, Jake and I talked with Detective Shawn Bryant for a bit. He was a nice-looking man with a masculine build. He conducted himself in a professional manner and had a strong personality though I could tell there was a softer side to him. He was not, at first, convinced something was wrong. It was a Sunday afternoon, he figured Mia went out to do errands or met up with a friend. It was not until he realized her cell phone was left at home with a text message from the middle of the night from an unknown number, stating whoever it was, was going to make her regret what she did. Then the Detective said it was certainly something to investigate and he recommended that we contact all friends, neighbors and family members of Mia's and he would put a search team together to look for her.

The kids, Mia's, and ours, were getting more worried by the minute. Jake and I knew we needed to be calm to keep them calm. This kind of thing does not happen in our neighborhood. After initially combing the neighborhood and closest surrounding areas nothing was found nor seemed indifferent which made all of us worry even more.

The other neighbors started helping by canvasing the adjacent streets. To my surprise, even Ava joined in. The police said they were going to contact Doug, but we never heard if had. It was now evening, and the fog started rolling in as we were expecting more storms throughout the night. A few of the neighbors stayed at our house, Andrea, Elizabeth and Grace, and the others went back home. We waited by the phone as the police were supposed to call us when or if they found Mia. Well, that call was never received.

It was getting late, and we all needed to get some sleep as we knew, but hoped not, that it would be a long day tomorrow. Mathew and Katy stayed at our house for the night.

FOUND

It was a sleepless night; we were still awake at dawn. No messages were left on any of our phones, no text messages...nothing from Mia. Mathew and Katy had gone to check if she had come home. Doug was there. He arrived in the middle of the night and knew the kids were with us. We all gathered at their house to discuss our next plan of action to try to find Mia. Suddenly, the police showed up with Detective Bryant. He did not have a pleasant look on his face. He told us they had found Mia, dead, in a ravine down a few blocks from our neighborhood. Doug and the kids were trembling and very distraught as were Jake, myself, and our kids. I could not believe the news; it did not seem real. How could this had happened? Why Mia? Who could had done this?

Jake and I, along with Andrew and Jolene, returned home in disbelief. The sun was shining, it was a beautiful warm summer day. How could the day be so perfect with what had happened? We were all incredibly quiet, none of us knew what to say. I could not believe we had just left Doug and the kids without Mia there. As I said, Mia and I rarely got together outside of the neighborhood, but I did consider her one of my best friends, if not the best. Aside from what was going on with her lately, we always had fun moments with one another.

The next day, we were told the condition in which Mia was found. She was strangled and half-naked. Detective Bryant said he had no doubt it was a homicide investigation now. He was waiting on the final autopsy report to confirm if she had been raped but there was evidence of her having sexual intercourse prior, which I would assume she would have had to have been raped since Doug was away on business. The detective said he would put a couple of patrol officers in our neighborhood for security reasons for a few nights to keep everyone at ease, but he felt this was not a random act. He was convinced Mia knew the person who killed her but why was he so sure of that?

The next couple of days were difficult as I was helping Doug with the final arrangements for Mia's funeral. He chose not to hold a wake for her but just a graveside ceremony.

On the day of Mia's funeral, it was a beautiful warm sunny day, just as it was on the day, she was found dead. Doug and Mia's families and friends were all there, Mathew and Katy's school friends were there and even all the neighbors showed up, except for one...Jeff. I had been so busy the last few days, I never even thought about him, and I had not seen him either. Detective Bryant also made an appearance but was not there to discuss the case.

After the funeral, there were no plans to have a gathering so we all just went our separate ways.

It had been several days since Mia had been buried and I had not heard any news from Detective Bryant or the police. The local tv news had nothing new to broadcast and the local newspaper had no new article about Mia's death. I had not heard anything from Doug either. I decided to contact Detective Bryant myself and find out the status of the case. He was more than willing to meet with me as he said Doug was not returning his calls.

The next morning, I met with the Detective at a small coffee shop in town. He asked if Mia had been having an affair as there was no evidence of her being raped prior to her death. I did not know how to answer that other than by saying no, but then I thought to myself, it was possible that she was. That would make sense why she had been acting so different lately, then I remembered the night she and Jeff were over for the barbecue, and I walked in on them having what seemed like an argument of some sort. I had to tell Detective Bryant what I saw and thought. He had other theories as well but did not divulge them to me at that time.

Later that evening, Doug called me. I was surprised to hear from him. He just wanted to thank me for helping with the funeral arrangements. I asked how he and the kids were doing and he said they were fine. To me, it seemed to me a little heartless, his response was not one I would have expected from a husband who had lost his wife and mother of his two children. But who was I to judge? I was not the one dealing with such a tremendous loss.

When Jake and I were getting ready for bed, we talked for a while. I wanted to know Jake's opinion on what had happened to Mia. He did not really have one, he was just going with what the police had said. I, on the other hand, thought more into it. There was something else, something the police or Detective Bryant may had been missing. "Why haven't we seen Jeff lately?" I asked Jake with curiosity. He replied, "Maybe he just isn't comfortable being around everything since he is new to the neighborhood." That made sense to me, I guess.

FAMILY AFFAIR

Weeks had passed, summer was ending, and the college kids were going back to school for the fall semester, including Mia's son. The neighborhood vibe was different since Mia's death. People were not out walking or running as much, and evenings were even quieter than usual. There were still so many unanswered questions, and the police still did not have any leads in the case. My want-to-be detective mode would kick in occasionally, but Jake would remind me often to leave the investigating to the real detectives. Then, one morning, Detective Bryant knocked on our door. It was early; I had not even had a cup of coffee yet. I invited him in, and he wanted to talk about Mia's case. He had questions he was hoping we could help answer, but Jake was at work, so it was only me. Detective Bryant asked if I knew a woman named April. I never knew anyone by that name, not even back in school. "Why?" I asked, "what does a woman named April have to do with this?" He answered, "I believe this woman April, whoever she is, was having an affair with Mia's husband." I was completely shocked, "Doug?" "I don't believe that!" I continued, "Doug is always away on business, he wouldn't have the time to have an affair." Detective Bryant responded with an even more shocking statement, "I believe this woman would accompany him on his business trips." I could not absorb what I was hearing. It never would have crossed my mind that Doug would be unfaithful. "Do you know anything more about this woman April?" I asked. He replied, "I only know her name because we found a note left in the hotel room Doug stayed in the night before Mai was found but I do have this photo of her from the hotel security camera." He then presented the photo to me, and it looked a lot like the woman I met at the neighborhood market, who said she was Jeff's sister. I again was in shock. "I've met her!" I said loudly, "this woman is the sister of my neighbor across the street." "You mean Jeff?" he asked. "Yes, Jeff, the one who I saw grabbing Mia's arm at my house that night." I had to take a moment before asking my next question. "Detective, what do you think there is a connection between them all?" He replied, "I am not sure as of yet, but I am going to figure that out soon."

For the next couple of days, I could not help but be consumed by this case. Jake kept recommending that I stay out of it and let Detective Bryant do his job. I just could not do that! Mia and Doug were friends of ours and their kids were friends of our kids. Their marriage seemed solid and there were never any indications they were having problems. Doug was away on business quite often, but he also provided a particularly good life for his family.

One afternoon, I saw Jeff out in his driveway, working on his motorcycle. I then decided to go across the street to talk to him. "Hi Jeff," I said as I was walking towards him, "we haven't seen you in a while." He put down his wrench and stood up. "I've been pretty busy lately," he replied, "what can I do for you?" he asked. "Well, I wanted to tell you I met your sister one day, at the neighborhood market." He looked at me with sort of a blank stare and responded with a question like comment, "Oh, you met April?" He did not follow that with another comment. I did not really know what else to say other than, "Well, she seemed very nice." I then thought it was best for me to just go back home so we left things as we would talk soon but as I started walking away, I turned back around quick to notice him calling someone on his cell phone and I assumed he was calling his sister.

The following day, I was looking out my kitchen window while washing dishes from breakfast when I saw a police car drive into Jeff's driveway. Two police officers got out of the car and were walking around the house and looking around the yard. I did not see if they entered his home. They were there for about twenty minutes or so, but I never saw Jeff. That prompted me to call Detective Bryant. He informed me they are investigating a lead they received, and it concerns Jeff, but he would not give me any further details. I did not want to think Jeff had anything to do with Mia's death, how could he? I thought he had just met Mia the same time I met him.

After speaking with the detective, I decided to go out for a walk. I ran into Ava, and she had lots of questions for me about Mia's death. I did not say much to her about it as I knew she would tell everyone in the neighborhood, and I did not have very much information anyway. After talking with her for a few minutes, I was fortunate enough to have Elizabeth and Grace come over to us. They were genuinely concerned about Doug and the kids. All I could tell them was they are doing okay under the circumstances and that there were no leads in the case. According to them, the neighbors were still worried about something like that happening again. I did let them know what Detective Bryant told me, that it was not a random murder. I just did not want them and the other neighbors to worry so much.

That night, I was sitting in my porch with Teddy, Jake was asleep, and the kids were out. I heard a noise. It sounded like a crash of some kind. Possibly trash cans falling over, a tree branch falling onto something or a car hitting a small object. Whatever it was, I wanted to wake Jake, but I decided to check it out on my own. When I was standing out on my front lawn, I heard the noise again. It sounded like it was coming from across the street, in Jeff's yard. I slowly walked across the street, a bit nervous, and as I was getting closer to his driveway, I saw Jeff walking out from his backyard. He saw me and asked what I was doing there. I told him I heard a noise, a couple of times and I

thought it was coming from his yard. He assured me he had not heard anything and that everything was fine over there. I then apologized for bothering him and said goodnight.

The next morning, I was about to get into my car to go to the bank when Jeff suddenly appeared in my driveway. He could tell he startled me. "I didn't mean to scare you; I know you were just about to leave but I wanted to apologize for last night." I took a moment before responding, "Oh, you don't need to apologize, I shouldn't have been out there that late anyway." He replied with a bit of a smile, "Well, most woman wouldn't be out that late alone, especially these days." I just looked at him and said, "I really need to get going, I have errands to run." I was uncomfortable after what he said and even more uncomfortable the way he said it. He went back across the street, and I quickly drove away. It had been more than a month since Mia's death, and no one had been arrested for her murder. I had not heard from Detective Bryant in days. Doug had been back to his regular work routine, going out of town on business trips but now with Mathew back at school, Katy was left alone. Jolene did go over there often to spend time with her, and we had her at our house quite a bit. I could not stop thinking that her father was out of town with Jeff's sister, and I could not stop thinking about Mia.

NEIGHBORHOOD GATHERING

It was time for our annual neighborhood fall festival when everyone gets together for a block party on the street. We all bring a dish for everyone to enjoy, and we have music as well as games for the younger children. This year, most of the neighbors joined in, except for Doug and the kids, which was understandable. To my surprise, Jeff was there, and he was there with the woman I once saw in his driveway, the brunette. I approached the two of them who were in a conversation with Ava at the time. "Excuse me, I'm sorry for interrupting." I said in the nicest tone I could as Ava smirked at me. "Well, I guess I will go mingle with the other neighbors." She said, as she was walking away which left just Jeff, the brunette and I standing there together. "Um, Jeff, I'm glad you decided to join in on our fall festival," I really did not know how to start the conversation I wanted to, but I continued, "and who is this?" I asked. Jeff replied quite quickly, "Oh, this is my fiancé, Lauren." Lauren chimed in right after, "Hi, it's nice to meet you." I interrupted, "It's Victoria, I live across the street from Jeff." The three of us had small talk, then went off in different directions. I was surprised Jeff had introduced Lauren as his fiancé since he never mentioned her to me or Jake before. I was sure she was the woman I saw that day in his driveway but why hadn't I seen her since? I assumed they broke up for a period.
Once the festival was over, some of the neighbors ended up gathering back at Andrea's house. I decided to stop by for a glass of wine. When I arrived, Jeff and Lauren were already there, laughing with the others and being quite affectionate to one another in front of everyone. They seemed happy but something to me was not sitting well. To me, it looked as if they were acting. Their actions did not seem genuine. I could not stand to watch any longer, so I just headed back home.

When I got home, I poured myself a glass of wine, since
I did not finish the one at Andrea's. I started to question
myself as to why I was so interested in Jeff's life. Yes,
when I first saw him across the street, I did think he was
very handsome and I will be honest, I did have a couple
of fantasies in my head about him but now, I was more
curious about who he was and what he was doing in our
neighborhood. I was beginning to not trust him and
question everything about him. He had not yet done any
repairs to his house and had not even started to do any
cleanup around the yard.

A KILLER AMONG US

Things around the neighborhood were beginning to get back to normal. It had been a couple of months since Mia's death, though there were still no arrest in the case, everyone seemed to be moving on with their lives and forgetting about what had happened to Mia. But not I. Doug had put the house on the market and there were constant open houses on the weekends. I did not want he and the kids to move. I felt if they did, I would lose any connection to Mia I once had. Doug did come to Jake and I before making the final decision to sell just to make us aware, so we were not surprised when we saw the for-sale sign on the front lawn. We understood his reasons to sell but we could not understand why he and the kids needed to move to a different state, many miles away.

Doug's house sold quickly as I knew it would. It was one of the most attractive houses on the street and one of the largest lots. I believe a family of five were moving in, but I had no desire to meet them right away as I still could not go over there since Mia died. It was still difficult to even drive by the house. A U-Haul was set in the driveway and Doug and Katy were loading it up with boxes. Doug hired a moving company to take care of the furniture and larger items. I was sitting out on my front porch when I noticed police vehicles pull up in their driveway. I then noticed Doug being taking away in handcuffs. Katy was screaming. I wanted so badly to run over to her but then I saw a woman officer take her into a separate car and both cars drove away. I was about to go into the house and call Jake when Detective Bryant pulled into my driveway. He quickly got out of his car and as he was walking up the stairs to my porch, he said, "We've made an arrest." I knew what was coming next. "We are charging Doug with Mia's murder." I was beyond shocked. "What?" I asked, "Why?" "Are you sure?" "Yes, we firmly believe based on latest evidence that Doug is Mia's killer," he answered in a professional tone. I could not believe what I was just told. My heart was breaking for Katy and Mathew. My heart was breaking for Mia, I know she would not have ever thought Doug would do something like that to her. Would we or could we ever think our spouse could or would ever do something like that? Could Jake ever do that to me?

It would not be long before all the neighbors and everyone in town were aware of Doug's arrest. Everyone had the same reaction. Everyone who knew Doug could not believe he would have been capable of doing such a horrific thing. Katy moved in with a distant relative of Mia's family in a town about twenty miles away. She no longer attended school with Jolene. Mathew was still in college and he and Andrew stayed connected over social media and text messages.

It would take a year before Doug's court trial would begin. Jake and I decided not to attend any of the proceedings as we did not want to hear about what had happened to Mia that night all over again. We should have been there to support the kids, but I could not bring myself to go there.
While the trial was in process, we did not see Jeff at all. He was not at home most days and nights. I had not seen his fiancé either. It seemed as if he would just stop by his house periodically but occasionally, I would notice a dim light coming from the basement window. Jake was constantly telling me to mind my own business, but I could not help but wonder why there would be a light on in the basement when Jeff did not appear to be home. After a long trial, Doug was found guilty. He was later sentenced to prison for life without the possibility of patrol. It was devastating news for all who still believed he was innocent, including myself and Jake. We, like most people, just never believed he was capable of such a thing despite all the evidence against him.
I still had not met the new neighbors who had moved into Doug's house, but I heard through the grapevine they were a young couple with three children, all under the age of five. They kept to themselves from the day they moved in. I did one day see Ava at their front door of course to introduce herself no doubt.

SURPRISE

The holidays were fast approaching and all the houses on the street were decorated with Christmas lights and such. Well, all but one...Jeff's house. I was not much in the holiday spirit, I still missed having coffee time and wine time with Mia and just talking with her. Her house was always beautifully decorated, one of the most festive in the neighborhood as she loved Christmas. Jake and I did not do too much with lighting, but we have always enjoyed decorating the trees in the front of our yard. Andrea and her husband Brad were hosting the neighborhood Christmas party this year, ironically, it should had been Doug and Mia's turn. We all decided not to dwell on the past that evening and just enjoy each other's company. The party was fun, Andrea and Brad did a wonderful job hosting. Right before the Yankee Swap was to begin, Jeff and his fiancé showed up. They brought gifts for the swap and a beautiful flower arrangement for Andrea. I went up to them both to say hello. I had to ask about the light I would often notice coming from the basement window. Jeff said it must be a loose bulb and he would check it out when he returned home. I also asked where he had been, and he just said he had been spending a lot of time at his fiancé's house in another town. His fiancé, Lauren, was quite talkative but Jeff was quiet. We never spoke of what happened or of his sister and Doug. He felt uncomfortable around me since I was the closest to Mia in the neighborhood.
It was New Year's Eve and Ava hosted that evening gathering every year. It was her thing since she did have the biggest house on the street if not in the neighborhood, but I will say she always did a remarkable job with the party. There were bartenders, cocktail servers, food caterers, even live entertainment. She certainly knew how to throw a party and it was always fun to celebrate on New Year's Eve with everyone, but this particular year was nothing like the past years. Aside from Mia being gone and Doug in prison, there were still many unanswered questions about that night and more curiosity about Jeff.

During the party, to everyone's surprise, Jeff's sister walked in. She looked like a supermodel, dressed in a gorgeous shimmering gold gown, down to her feet, with a stunning diamond neckline. Her dangling diamond earrings were glistening against her blonde up do. Everyone just had to stare at her for a moment, not just because of how striking she looked but because everyone knew she was the one who Doug had the affair with. Ava came running over to welcome her and from what I could hear of their conversation, she invited her. I was not aware of their friendship until that moment. The rest of the evening was a little awkward. You could hear people whispering and we all knew the whispers were about April. I could not believe she had the gall to show up at a party on the street knowing Doug and Mia's neighbors would be there. Other than mingling with Ava, she stayed next to Jeff and Lauren for the rest of the evening. I had consumed enough wine for one night so following the "Happy New Year" celebration toast, Jake and I left the party and went home.

The next morning, I was eating breakfast at my kitchen table when I heard yelling outside. It sounded like an argument of some sort. I got up to look out my kitchen window and I saw Jeff and his sister screaming at one another. It was none of my business, but I personally had never heard siblings argue like they were. They were very loud. I saw April slap Jeff in the face, and I saw him push her right after. I was going to go over there to settle things down, but then I felt I should not get myself involved. Shortly after, the arguing stopped, and April drove away in a new Mercedes.

I went back to continue eating my breakfast when suddenly there was a loud, hard knock on my front door. I quickly got up to answer it, not expecting who would be on the other side. It was Jeff. He said to me in an angry voice with an angry look, "I would appreciate it Victoria, if you would stop being so concerned with my life!" I did not know how to respond to that. It took me a minute to absorb what he had just said to me and how he said it. "I'm sorry Jeff, I don't know what you're talking about." He replied in an aggravated tone, "You are always spying on me through your kitchen window or from your porch, you are always asking questions that you don't need to know the answers to. What I do across the street is my own business!" At that point, I was embarrassed because I knew he was not wrong. I had been constantly looking across the street and prying for information about him. "I apologize for my behavior Jeff," I said sincerely, "I promise I will no longer be so distracted by you." I did have to chuckle a second after I said that, but it made him calm down because he chuckled a bit, too. I agreed to be just a friendly neighbor from across the street. Though, I knew at that moment, we would not be having any more barbecues with him. When I told Jake what had happened, he agreed as well that we would both just be friendly neighbors, acquaintances rather than friends.
Months had passed and winter was ending. It had been quite a long time since I had seen Detective Bryant because why would I have seen him anyway? Doug was in prison for Mia's murder, the case was closed.

It was Monday, around nine o'clock in the morning. I received a phone call from Detective Bryant asking if he could stop by as he had something he wanted to tell me, and he did not want to tell me over the phone. About an hour later, he arrived at my house. He came in and I poured him a cup of coffee. "Is there something wrong?" I asked him. "Well, there was a woman found in the ravine a few blocks away from here," he continued to say, "the same location we found Mia." I was shocked, "Why are you telling me this?" I asked. Detective Bryant paused for a moment before answering my question. "She was found in the same manner as Mia, strangled and half-naked." I put my hand over my mouth for a second before responding. "That's awful, what a coincidence." He then stated, "I don't believe it is a coincidence...the woman we found is April." "April? the woman who Doug had the affair with? Jeff's sister? That April?" I asked in a frantic voice. Detective Bryant confirmed it was April, but her last name was not Stevens, like Jeff's. Something else I did not know until that moment. Her last name was Higgins. I asked the detective what connection he thought there might be between the two identical murders. He said he did not have enough information yet to make that connection. The neighborhood was once again going to be in a panic. I did ask Detective Bryant if he thought Doug was innocent after all or if this was just a copycat killing. He did not want to comment on that without more evidence. I now wanted to run across the street and see if Jeff was okay as Detective Bryant said he had just been told earlier in the morning about what had happened, but I knew it was best for me to stay away.

After the detective left, I called Jake at work to let him know the news. We talked about it for a while when he got home. By then, it had been all over the media and throughout the neighborhood. Andrew and Jolene had questions that we could not answer. So many what ifs were going through my mind, but I did not feel unsafe, nor did I worry about the safety of my kids. I knew these horrible events must be connected in ways not related to my family or most of the other neighbors for that matter. I just could not figure out why Mia then April...and both had a connection with Doug. Again, Jake had to remind me to let the police do their jobs.
The next evening, I was sitting out on my front porch finishing my glass of wine from dinner and I saw Jeff pull into his driveway. I knew Jake was watching tv in the upstairs den, so I decided to walk across the street. Just as Jeff was getting off his motorcycle, I stood behind, at a loss for words for a moment, especially because of our conversation. "Um, Jeff...I just wanted to say how sorry I am to hear about April." He gave a look that showed me he knew I was being sincere and replied, "Thank you...I appreciate that." There were a couple of minutes of silence. I should have then walked away but I did not. "I can't imagine what you are going through so if you need anything or just need to talk, please come to me." He responded in a surprised tone, "I will." I then turned around to walk back across the street when Jeff stopped me and said, "Victoria...be careful." I did not respond with any words, I just stared at him for a minute then continued to walk back to my house.
I was feeling a little uneasy because of what Jeff had last said to me and because the way he said it. I did not want to tell Jake since he would not have wanted me to go over there in the first place.

INDISCRETIONS

A few days had passed, and everything was quiet in the neighborhood. The media had lightened up on April's story. There was no current information to report. I needed to go out and run some errands and when I returned, I noticed Detective Bryant's car in Jeff's driveway. About an hour later, it was gone. It was strange he did not stop by to see me as he had always done if he was in the neighborhood for any reason. A few minutes after Detective Bryan left, there was a knock on my door. It was Jeff. He looked worried and a little sad. "You said if I needed to talk, I could come to you." I reluctantly invited him in, "Yes, of course, please, come in." I decided it was best to sit and talk out back on the patio for more privacy. Jake was at work and the kids were both at school. I offered coffee or tea at first but then realized since it was after noontime, I also offered beer or wine. He opted for a beer, so naturally I poured myself a big glass of wine. Not much was said at first, we both just sat there for a while then Jeff began talking about April. He became visibly upset while telling me all about her and her life as if he felt responsible for what had happened to her. I began to feel his pain and that is when I realized he and I had connected with one another.

We sat out on the patio for what seemed like hours, and we talked more than I have talked with Jake in some time. I was finally getting to know Jeff...almost in an intimate way. We stopped talking about April and were having conversations about our younger years and life in general. There were quite a few laughs between us and a few more beers and glasses of wine. It was getting later in the afternoon but the way we were looking at each other, we both knew we had so much more to talk about. When I stated Andrew and Katy would be home from school soon, Jeff asked if I wanted to continue our conversations at his house. I hesitantly said yes but knew I could not just tell my kids I was going to continue drinking and hanging out with the handsome younger man across the street so I decided to tell them I was going out for a long walk to clear my head and I would not be home until close to dinner time since I knew Jake would be home by that time anyway.

I walked over to the street behind Jeff's house knowing I could get to his backyard that way, which was very overgrown and not maintained at all, and he meant me at the gate. He had a full glass of wine waiting for me, ironically the brand I drink, and he was holding a snifter of something which I found out was whiskey. Things seemed quite different between us suddenly since it felt like we were doing something wrong. It had become a little chilly and breezy, so he wrapped his sweatshirt around me. At this point, I was beginning to feel guilty just being there with him but excited at the same time, though I knew it was time for me to leave. As I was heading out the back gate, Jeff insisted we get together again soon, and I agreed to do so.

As I returned home from my "walk," Jake was just pulling into the driveway. "Hey honey, where'd you go, out for a run?" I took a minute to answer him, "Uh, no, I went for a long walk around the neighborhood and such." I felt awful for not telling him the truth but how could I? It certainly would not have gone over well. Although Jake and Jeff did get along quite well when we had Jeff over that day for the barbecue, I would not be able to explain this little get together we had without him.

Later that evening, while we were getting ready for bed, Jake received a text message from a colleague at work asking if he could attend a seminar the following week for a few days. It happened to also be the week Andrew would be away on a camping trip with his friends from school and Katy had plans to stay at her best friends' family beach house. Jake did not go away for work very often so he was concerned that I may be upset about him leaving but I assured him, I was not, and I told him he should go. What came to my mind was not he and the kids being away but being home alone for a few days...with the handsome young man across the street. The man I had just had drinks and conversations with, secretly, and I knew I wanted to do it again. I had been intrigued by him for a while now. Since the day he moved in, I had a desire to know him, and I found myself thinking about him all the time. If only I had listened to Jake from the beginning. I had become that nosey neighbor, but after spending time with Jeff earlier in the day, I wanted to spend more time with him, and I knew I now had my chance since I would be alone for a few days during the week.

The next morning, I did go out for a legitimate run. Jeff was on his motorcycle driving down our street and he stopped to say hello. I do not know why I was so quick to tell him about Jake and the kids, but I did. "Um, Jeff...Jake and the kids will all be away for a few days next week so I thought we could pick up where we left off yesterday." I was eagerly awaiting his response. "Sure, that sounds great!" He seemed excited. "Would you prefer my place or yours?" That was something I had not thought about yet but I

answered quickly anyway, "How about my house?" I figured it would be better to control things in my own environment or at least I hoped it would be. We made our plans and went our separate ways. I was no longer focused on my run; in fact, it was difficult to even run. Instead, I switched to a slow leisurely gait and began imagining what could happen between Jeff and I and in my head it did not seem wrong.

Jake had left for his work seminar and Andrew left a couple of hours later then Katy was picked up by her friend soon after. It was nearing dinner time. When I looked out my kitchen window, I could see Jeff in his driveway working on his motorcycle wearing his infamous wife beater t-shirt and dark blue jeans that could not fit anyone else better. His hair had the messy look, which was common for him with his thick, curly hair. I just stood there staring as I have so many times. I wanted so much to go across the street and invite him over, but then I did not have to...because he was walking up to my front door.

When I answered the door, Jeff was a little sweaty as it was humid outside. His skin had a shiny appearance and the definition of his muscles, well, I could have just stared at him all night. He asked with his huge smile if I had a wrench he could borrow and then chuckled. I giggled back and realized that was just his way of breaking the ice so to speak and making light of the moment. We also knew it would not hurt to have an excuse ready if any of the neighbors saw him at my door or enter my house.

We both sat on the sofa in the living room, I put on the gas fireplace for a little ambiance. I brought in a bottle of wine which he opened and poured for us.

Conversation began quickly, we were laughing and enjoying the evening. He seemed interested in every word I said and the way he looked at me when I laughed seemed so intense. The more I was really getting to know him, the more I felt I did not really know him at all. There was still something about him that kept me asking myself if he was as perfect as he seemed to be. Though, now, it did not seem to matter much.

There was a point where we just stopped talking for a bit. I could tell he was in deep thought for a moment. His eyes were a little glossy as if he were about to cry. I asked him what was wrong, and he put his arms around me and hugged me close for what felt like a long time but was only a few minutes. "Are you okay, Jeff?" I asked in a concerning voice. He paused, looked into my eyes, and kissed me. I kissed him back. After a couple of minutes, things began to get heated and as we were laying back on the sofa, I knew in my head what I was doing was completely wrong, but I was so into the moment and what was happening I could not seem to stop, nor did I want to, but he then suddenly did. "I can't do this; I am sorry Victoria" he said as he was getting up from the sofa. He then abruptly left. I just sat there wondering what changed his mind. It was an awkward moment. Part of me felt self-conscious while part of me felt relieved things did not go further. I knew it would feel strange seeing him again which I did the next morning.

Jeff was outside actually mowing the lawn, so I decided to walk over there with a couple cups of coffee. After being up most of the night, dwelling on what had happened between the two of us and what didn't, I thought I would just deal with it and get it out of the way. "Good morning" I said loudly as I was walking toward him. He turned off the mower. I handed him a cup of coffee, "I figured I would come over to apologize for last night." He thanked me for the coffee and replied, "Victoria, it was not your fault, it was mine." He continued, "I should not have started something that you probably are not even sure about." I quickly responded, "What I chose to do or not do is my choice Jeff, you did not force me into anything." He gave me a smile. "Well, I know I want to be with you again and this time I

don't want to stop." I was surprised and excited though I felt extremely guilty for what I was about to say next, "Me too." We then made plans to get together again at my house that evening but this time I would make dinner.

It was close to six o'clock and Jeff was due to arrive
soon. I put on a black tight-fitting dress and put my hair
up in a bun. I wore my favorite red lipstick and felt as if
I were getting ready for a real date, butterflies, and all
but then the guilt would set in, and I would think about
Jake and the kids. I was about to cancel the whole thing
when Jeff arrived right on time. He looked so handsome
wearing a white collared dress shirt with the first three
buttons undone, exposing his bare chest, and a dark
navy suit jacket and those jeans, I love the jeans he
wears. I was feeling like a high school girl all over again,
well, more like a college student.

Dinner was delicious. We started with salad and rolls. For the main course, I made a vegetable lasagna, a family recipe my mom made when I was growing up. I had not made it for quite some time as Jake did not particularly care for Italian food. For dessert, Jeff had brought over a small red velvet cake for the two of us to share. The evening seemed so normal, even though it was not normal at all and not with my husband. I had concluded I must have underlying issues with my marriage that I have been ignoring since I did not feel any guilt being with Jeff. Immediately after dinner, before dessert, I received a text message. It was from Jake. He was just checking in and said he could not call because he was at a work dinner. He ended his text with "I Love You." Now, I was feeling guilty but did not let it end my evening with Jeff. After dessert, we moved into the living room and things began to progress, one thing leading to another, and we made our way upstairs into the spare bedroom. My bedroom was off limits. We took things slow at first, but it quickly turned into an aggressive act of lovemaking. He was gentle yet strong and I allowed myself to be completely controlled by him. When we finished, no words were spoken for what seemed like a long time but we just both lied there in each other's arms. Then I had to ask, "What have we done?...What do we do now?" He quietly said, "We do what you want us to do." He knew my feelings were different now than they were before we did this, but I did not know what my feelings were. I was thinking about Jake, but I was also thinking about Jeff, and the next time we could be together like this.

Jeff did not spend the night as I felt it would not be appropriate, though did that even matter now. He stayed for another couple of hours, and we sat downstairs at the kitchen table and finished the bottle of wine from dinner, and we acted as if what just had happened between us, did not. Again, everything seemed so normal.

It was late, and Jeff was getting ready to leave. His shirt was unbuttoned, and he had his jacket draped over his shoulder. As we said goodbye at the front door, which was opened half-way, he kissed me goodnight and said he would see me the next day. As he was walking down the stairs, Ava was walking by with her dog. She stopped and stared at Jeff and then me in the doorway. I was so shocked to see her or any neighbor for that matter and I was scared because I knew she obviously knew Jeff was leaving from my house and his shirt was wide opened. At that moment, I did not know if I should acknowledge her there or ignore her and shut my door. Jeff said hello to her and kept walking across the street. I then just looked at her briefly, turned around, went into my house, and closed the door. I saw her still standing there when I looked out the sidelight of the door. I then shut off my porch light and tried not to worry about what she saw. Though, I knew she of all people would not let something like that go without confronting me about it very soon.

The next day, I was waiting for Ava to show up on my doorstep all day which she had not done yet. Just when I thought she did not think too much about what she saw, she arrived at my house. I met her on the front porch. "Well, where's Jake these days?" she asked as if it was any of her business. "He's away at a work seminar." "And the kids?" she asked curiously. "Andrew is camping with friends and Jolene is away friends as well." I was getting agitated. "Ava, if there is something you'd like to say, just say it!" She responded, "No, there isn't...I just thought it was a little strange that Jeff would be coming out of your house at such a late hour last night." I knew I needed to reply quickly with something to deter her from thinking the truth, "Oh yes, well, I had a leak under the kitchen sink and Jeff was coming home from a night out so I caught him in his driveway and asked if he could stop over and try to repair it for me since Jake is out of town." I could not believe how fast I was able to think of that excuse. I went from being an adulterer to being a good liar all within a matter of hours and it seemed clear to me that Ava believed me. I was no longer worried about her saying anything to anyone which was a terrible thing since I was prepared to let my guard down again.

Jeff and I made plans to see each other again, one more time before Jake and the kids were all due to come home. It was early evening and he made dinner reservations for us at a secluded quiet and romantic restaurant out of town. We met each other there. We had a wonderful dinner, and we were so comfortable with one another. It was as if we were meant to be together. After dinner, I left my car in the parking lot while Jeff and I went out for a ride on his motorcycle. He brought me to a beach along the highway. It was such a beautiful, calm, warm evening. We walked along the beach and sat in the sand for a while and just talked. We held hands and kissed quite a bit. It felt so good to be with him again. We both knew it would be the last time we would have a moment like that since life would have to go back to the way it was...or would it?

The next day, Jake returned home early from his seminar. Andrew came back a little later and Jolene was due to come home the following day. Within minutes, everything seemed so-called normal again as if the past few days never happened, though I could not forget that they did. I was trying hard not to make Jake think something was up or to alert him to anything, but I could not stop thinking about Jeff Weeks had gone by and still every time I walked by the spare bedroom, I would stop and just stare at the bed for a minute and smile. I had not spoken to Jeff since our night at the beach and I missed him. I really missed him. When I saw him leave his house one morning on his motorcycle after not seeing him for a while, I wanted to just run out and jump on the back of his bike and tell him to take me away and that is when I realized I really did want to be with him. But then I realized, we had never talked about his fiancé, Lauren. Why was she never brought up in our conversations we had? Why did I allow myself to get involved with someone who is engaged to be married? Why was I unfaithful with someone who was also unfaithful? I could not stop thinking about her now. I was not even thinking about Jake. I had fallen in love with a man who I would never be with again.
Jeff had given me his cell phone number after our first get together and I had been contemplating texting him about Lauren for days now. So, I did. He did not respond right away but later he did. He replied by saying, well, texting, that he and she had decided to call off their engagement due to her accepting a job offer several hours away. I was so excited to read that. He then texted and asked about Jake. I just put a question mark because I did not understand what he was asking. He then texted stating he wanted to know if I was planning to leave Jake. Things suddenly got real. Too real for me to manage at that moment so I just replied with a red heart emoji and texted that I missed him.

HIDDEN AGENDA

For the next several days, I was constantly thinking about my life with Jake, our kids, the neighborhood, and Jeff. I wanted to be with him so badly but at the same time, I did not want to leave my husband. I did not want to leave my secure life. I did not want to break my family apart. I wanted to be with Jeff but knew I could not have it all. I also knew Jeff would not just sit around and wait for me and he deserved to know what my plans were.

It was Valentine's Day. Jake always brings home a bouquet of spring-colored flowers with a box of my favorite chocolates from a confectioner in town. I receive the same gifts every year along with a hallmark card that I know he does not actually read before buying. But this year, I received another gift. It was left on my porch swing. A dozen of long-stemmed yellow roses, which are my favorite flowers and color. I knew they were from Jeff, and I was amazed he remembered that from a conversation we had the night at the beach. He was careful and left them when he knew Jake and the kids would not be home. I only wish I saw him leave them so I could bring him into the house and that would not have been a rational idea. I knew I would later have to tell Jake and the kids I bought the roses for myself as a little pick me up.

As March was approaching, the weather was still a little cool, but our weather is generally nice all year round. I had not seen much of Jeff lately. We had been texting back and forth every now and then since Valentine's but have not had any chance to get together. I still missed him so much.

It was Wednesday afternoon, and I had the tv on in the kitchen. The five o'clock news came on with a breaking story. A woman's body was found in a reservoir near our neighborhood and then I realized it was the same location Mia and April's bodies were found in. I dropped my kitchen knife to the floor and frantically called Jake on my cell phone. I was scared because now I knew this must be the same person who killed Mia...and killed April. After speaking with Jake, I called Detective Bryant. He did not have any information other than what had already been disclosed on the news. I told him I was frightened and worried for the safety of myself, my daughter, and the other women in the neighborhood. He assured me he would put this latest death his priority and would update me with any added information. I then went over to see Andrea, Elizabeth, Grace and yes, even Ava as it was important to let them know about what I just seen on the news in case they were not aware. I then later went to stop by Jeff's but noticed his motorcycle was gone so I knew he was not home. As I was sitting out on my front porch, Jeff drove into his driveway. I ran over to him, his bike still running. "Jeff!" I said loudly, "Did you hear, another body was found in the ravine where Mia and April were found?" He responded, "Yes, I did...It was Lauren." He did not seem as upset as I would have expected him to be, I assumed it was because he was in shock. "Oh my god, Jeff, I am so sorry, I had no idea. They did not release her name on the news." I then hugged him, and he kissed me on the neck, a few times. I did not want to let go but I knew since we were standing in the driveway, it was possible others could see us. As I turned around, I noticed Jake coming down the street. I wanted to get back home before he saw me with Jeff, but he made it there before me. So, I needed to act very casual. "Jake," I was getting his attention while he was getting out of his truck, "the body they found in the reservoir was Lauren's, Jeff's ex-fiancé." Jake was as shocked as I was. "You're kidding!" "Did you contact Detective Bryant?" he asked. "Yes, I already did. He couldn't tell me anything, he is just beginning to work on the case." Then Jake asked overly concerned, "Do they think it was the same person who killed Mia and April?" "I don't know," I said, "I don't know."

Jake knew I was distraught about Lauren, but he did not know one of the many reasons was because I was worried about Jeff. Even though, he and Lauren were no longer engaged, my heart ached for him, and I wanted so much to go across the street to console him. Although he did not seem terribly upset when we spoke about it, I knew he must be hurting. We were all hurting within the neighborhood in some way because it had been the third homicide in a brief period, close to home and involved women...but what was the connection?

It was a Sunday afternoon and despite the recent murder of Lauren, Ava was having a cook-out at her house for a few of the neighbors. I guess Jake and I were lucky we made the list of those invited. I was not thrilled about attending but it was a nice afternoon, the weather was perfect, and Jake wanted to go. He said it would be a good distraction, to help get our minds off Lauren's death.

When we arrived, Jeff was already there talking with Andrea's husband Greg and Tom,

Grace's husband. Jake had gravitated toward them while I went over to talk with Grace and Andrea. I was trying my hardest not to keep staring over at Jeff, but we managed to continue to keep eye contact with each other. I asked where Elizabeth and Dave were and Andrea said their youngest child, Molly, was not feeling well. Michael, Ava's husband was putting hamburgers and hot dogs on the grill, everyone seemed to be having an enjoyable time. Lots of beer and wine always helps. Suddenly, Ava came over to the three of us. "Hello ladies, are you all enjoying yourselves?" Grace responded to her, "Yes, Ava, as always, it's a wonderful cook-out, thank you for inviting all of us." "Well, as you know I enjoy entertaining..." Then came what I should have expected from her. "So, Victoria, are you having any more problems with your kitchen sink?" Jake had overheard what Ava asked me as the guys were not standing too far from us and he came right over. "What problem with the kitchen sink?" I quickly answered, "Oh yes, the kitchen sink was leaking a bit a while back" Ava interrupted me, "Jake, you were away on business or something." I wanted so badly to slap her in the face, but I knew I had to keep calm and think of what I was going to say next but then Jeff quickly added to the conversation. "Yea, Jake, Victoria asked me to come over and look at it, so I did. It was a lose pipe fitting underneath that I tightened. No big deal." I was so relieved Jeff intervened. Jake thanked him for helping and Ava certainly did not achieve what I know she sought out to do. "Well," she then continued with what I know was meant to be a snide remark "it's nice to have neighbors who are always willing to help when needed." Then she walked away.

The rest of the afternoon was relaxing. Jeff and I spoke briefly when Jake went to grab another beer. He whispered in my ear, "I want to see you later." I whispered back, "I don't know how I can." Then Jake returned and we just started talking about the weather. We had all eaten way too much food and drank too much beer and wine and everyone seemed to be having fun, but it was getting late, and Jake was tired. He wanted to get back home. I was struggling to figure out how I could meet Jeff later but then realized it would be impossible. I later texted Jeff to let him know I could not see him since Jake was home, but I asked in the text if we could meet at the beach he took me to before and since Jake would be at work and the kids in school, I knew it would be safe. He texted back with a red heart emoji and typed CAN'T WAIT!

When I came to bed, Jake was still up watching tv. He asked "Hey, why didn't you tell me about Jeff needing to fix our sink?" I was a little nervous, "Oh, I just forgot about it. You were away and when you got home it just didn't cross my mind." He responded, "Well, I'll take a look at it tomorrow, to make sure it doesn't leak again." He then put his arm around me and started to caress my breasts, but I abruptly stopped him. "Jake, I'm tired. It's been a long day." He just gave a heavy sigh and turned over. I knew I could not have sex with him while I was thinking about my upcoming plans with Jeff.

The next morning when I got out of bed the house was empty. I was confused as to what I should wear, Jeff and I were meeting at the beach, so I obviously wanted to wear lite clothing. I was so excited to be with him again. I threw my hair up in a ponytail and did not wear much makeup which I don't anyway unless I am going out at night.

I drove to the beach and arrived a few minutes earlier
than Jeff. I waited in my car in a lot close to where he
had parked his motorcycle back when we were there
before. He pulled right up to my driver's side door, got
off his bike and grabbed a bag from his seat
compartment. I grabbed a blanket from the trunk, and
we walked while holding hands to a secluded spot on the
beach behind a large rock. I put down the blanket,
spreading it out for both of to lay on and he opened the
bag he was carrying and inside was a bottle of wine, a
single yellow rose, and a package of strawberries. It was
so sweet. He looked at me and said, "You are beautiful
Victoria." I acted a little shy and was blushing, "Oh Jeff,
you are...," then I lost my train of thought and leaned in
to kiss him. We kissed for a long time and then as
before, one thing led to another, and we were making
love on the beach. Not even concerned if others were
around, as we were hidden behind a large rock
surrounded by shrubs and bushes. When we were
finished, we just held one another tightly and told each
other we never wanted this thing between us, whatever
it was, to end, and that was the moment I realized I
needed to leave Jake.

As we walked back to the lot where we had both been
parked, we noticed a vehicle parked across from us. The
car's engine was running and there was a man in the
driver's seat. He had a baseball cap on and dark
sunglasses. We could not really see his face, but he
seemed to have been just sitting there staring at us, as
if he had been waiting for us. Jeff and I looked away and
continued to walk to my car. He then drove away. We
both agreed it was a little odd and neither of us
recognized the car.

Before we went our separate ways, I asked Jeff to be
patient with me as I needed some time before telling
Jake I was going to leave him. I had so much more at
stake, really, than Jeff since I was only one with
children. I did not even have a job. My life would change
drastically, and I was terrified. Jeff assured me if would
give me the time I needed but he did make it clear he
was not going to wait too long.

For the next week or so, I mostly kept to myself. I did not sit out on my front porch to avoid seeing any of the neighbors as I knew I would soon be the talk of the neighborhood. Jake was constantly asking me if anything was wrong because I had been so quiet toward him and the kids. I would often look out my kitchen window to get a glimpse of Jeff across the street and whenever I saw him, I was sure of what I wanted to do. I just did not know how to do it. I was worried about what Jake would do and how Andrew and Jolene would handle it and what they would then think of me. Would they ever forgive me for breaking up our family? Would Jake be able to continue to live in our house across the street from Jeff...and me? And then I wondered if Jeff intended on having me move right in with him. Then it dawned on me that Jeff and I had not discussed any of that. I thought to myself, shouldn't I know what his plans were before we disrupt everyone's lives? So, I knew I needed to talk with Jeff before I told Jake about us.

CHANGE OF PLANS

It was an early Saturday morning. The kids had both left for the day. Jake and I were having coffee in the kitchen. It seemed like the perfect time to tell him about me and Jeff. We had been distant from each other for weeks now and I assumed he sensed something was going on with me. I was nervous, a bit shaky, but it was time. Until I met Jeff, I never once thought of ever leaving Jake. I had no reason to. We had been together since college, and he had always been a great husband and father. As I stated in the beginning, we had built a solid life here in the neighborhood and had formed many friendships along the way with other couples and families. I was now comparing myself to Doug since he had an affair. I did not feel good about myself for what I had been doing but my heart, and my desire, took over and I just wanted to be with Jeff all the time. I was completely willing to give up all that I had for him.

I was about to start my conversation about Jeff when Jake saw blue lights flashing out the kitchen window. He abruptly got up from his seat and said in an anxious sounding voice, "Hey, there are cop cars next door!" I jumped up and ran to the kitchen window and noticed three police cruisers in Jeff's driveway. Jake and I ran out to the front porch and that is when we saw Jeff in handcuffs being put into the back of one of the cruisers. I was devastated! I started to cry, and Jake asked why I was so upset. I could only answer him by saying it was traumatizing to see a neighbor being arrested. I had no idea what was going on. I wanted so much to run across the street and ask what was happening, but I knew it was not my place to do so.

I did not get much sleep that night as I was so worried about Jeff. Jake knew I was too. I wanted to know why he was arrested, and I did not want to sit around and wait for Detective Bryant to contact me.

PRESUMED INNOCENT

The following morning, I had to call Detective Bryant to find out what was happening with Jeff. He agreed to meet me at the police station later that morning. I told Jake I needed to get some groceries as I did not want him to know I was going to meet with the Detective. When I arrived, Detective Bryant and I went into his office, and we started to talk about Jeff's arrest. He said they had enough evidence to connect Jeff to the three recent murders. I was in total disbelief. Then Detective Bryant asked me why I was so concerned. I had to tell him. It felt as if a huge weight had been lifted off me. Detective Bryant looked surprised by what I told him, and I did not hold anything back. I told him there was no way Jeff could be the killer. I knew him and I knew him well now. It could not have been him. Detective Bryant told me he was not completely convinced Jeff was the killer, but he had to go with the evidence on hand. All three women, he said, had a connection to Jeff and he believed none of the murders were random. He told me he was sure each of them was specifically targeted. I knew April had a connection to Jeff because she was his sister, and I knew Lauren did because she was his ex-fiancé but what was his connection to Mia?

When I returned home from my "shopping trip," Jake was sitting out on the front porch waiting for me. I had only stopped at a convenience store to grab a few items rather than the large grocery store but I had my own shopping bag so it would not have looked suspicious. He seemed a little agitated. "Victoria, I think we need to talk." I was getting nervous. "Oh, sure, about what?" I asked, trembling inside. "I want to know why you were so visibly upset when you saw Jeff being arrested." I paused for a minute. "Jake, I already told you...it was because I was shocked, that's all." I continued, "It is always upsetting to see a neighbor or friend in trouble." Jake did not say anything for a couple of minutes, then he said with somewhat of an angry tone, "maybe one day, Victoria, I will find out the real reason." He then turned around to walk away and I yelled "Jake, wait!" but he went back into the house and slammed the door behind him. I was getting worried that he suspected or even knew more than I had thought. Could he have been aware of my affair with Jeff? Regardless, I was more concerned for Jeff as he was being held in jail while Detective Bryant searched for more evidence to pin against him or hopefully to clear him.

For the next few days, Jake and I did not really talk to each other much and when we did, it was always with a bit of a snippy tone. It was becoming quite uncomfortable, for both of us, I think. It was Wednesday and I had not heard anything from Detective Bryant since Sunday so with Jake at work and the kids in school, I decided to go down to the police station. When I arrived, I saw Detective Bryant coming out of the building. I ran over to him. "Detective Bryant!" He stopped walking. "Hi Victoria, what can I do for you?" "Well, I was just wondering if there were any new leads in the case?" He paused. "No, not yet but I assure you I am doing nothing but focusing all my attention to this case." I smiled and nodded my head. "Um, I was also wondering if I could see Jeff?" He looked away briefly. "Victoria, Jeff had already advised us not to let you see him...I'm sorry." My heart hurt when he said those words. "Oh," I said as a tear rolled down my cheek. "Ok...thank you Detective, for putting so much effort into this case." I started to walk away, and Detective Bryant said, "Victoria, if Jeff is innocent, I will find the guilty one, I promise you that." I gave him a little finger wave and walked back to my car.

The weekend was here, and Grace and Tom were having a cocktail party at their house. Jake was going but I decided not to. He was unhappy about my decision, but I knew I could not attend and act like everything was okay, nor did I want to hear all the gossip and rumors about Jeff. Instead, I planned to just sit out in my backyard with Teddy and a glass of wine in front of the firepit and that is exactly what I did while writing a letter to Jeff.

It was late and Jake had not yet come back from the party. It was unusual that he would stay so late but under the circumstances, he obviously wanted to be over there than home with me. I understood completely. I must have fallen asleep on my lounger, cuddled up under a blanket with Teddy because I awoke to Jake telling me to get inside and go to bed. I grabbed my empty glass of wine and headed in.

The next morning, I realized Jake must not have slept in our bed the night before since his side of the bed had not been undone. When I walked by our spare bedroom, the bed was not made as it was the day before. I came downstairs and he was sitting at the kitchen table having coffee. I said good morning and he just gave me a disgusted look and then threw a piece of paper at me which I then remembered was the letter I had started to write to Jeff. I obviously left it outside near my lounger. I did not know what to say or do. Jake read the letter and he now knew. "I'm sorry Jake, I'm sorry." That was all I could think of saying to him at that moment. He got up from the table and said harsh words with so much anger towards me. "I hope you lie comfortable in the bed that you've made!" Before he walked out of the house, he told me he would be gone for the next few days, but he would be back later to grab some things. I certainly did not want Jake to find out about Jeff this way, but he refused to talk about it, so I had no choice but to leave him alone and let him deal with it in whatever way he needed to. I was not going to tell Andrew or Jolene anything yet and I knew Jake did not want to either, at least not until we were able to make decisions together as to what we would do next.
So, I decided to write a new letter to Jeff. I wanted to deliver it personally to Detective Bryant as I trusted him to give it to Jeff. I just wanted him to know I believed in his innocence and that I still love him.

Dear Jeff,

I am thinking about you, I have not stopped for a minute. My heart is breaking more each day that I cannot be with you. Jake knows about us now. I want you back home so I can kiss you and we can stop hiding from the world. I know you are innocent, the man I have fallen in love with would not be capable of such violence. You have made me feel so special and I am willing to give up everything I have or had to spend the rest of my life with you. I will be here waiting for you to come back to me when this horrible situation is over. You do not belong in jail; you belong here with me.
I love you,

Victoria

A few days later, Detective Bryant stopped by to give me a letter from Jeff. I was so excited and could not wait to read it. I poured a glass of wine and went upstairs to the spare bedroom. I lied on the bed and opened the letter.

Hey Beautiful!

I too have not stopped thinking about you or about us. You are the reason I refuse to rot in here for something I did not do. You must believe me! I did not do any of this! I have made mistakes, many that cannot be fixed but I did not kill Lauren, April, or Mia. I love you Victoria, please help me, please!

Jeff

I felt even more helpless after reading his letter. I wanted so badly to hold him, and it hurt so much not to know when I would ever hold him again or if I even would. Just as I was about to walk out of the bedroom while wiping the tears from my face, Jake was standing there in the doorway, staring at me. "Is he even worth it?" he asked ignorantly. I answered him honestly, "Yes Jake, he is." He chuckled and said to me, "Well, he may never get himself out of jail so really Victoria, you may have broken this family apart for nothing!" He may had been right, but I was so hoping he would be wrong. "I don't want to argue with you Jake, if you'd prefer, I will be the one to leave." He then said "No, I will be leaving...soon...but Andrew and Jolene will be coming with me." Now things were starting to get too complicated and hurtful. I knew I would face consequences for my actions though I did not consider my children and what they would now have to endure because of my bad choices which still had not felt so bad. I told Jake we should allow both Andrew and Jolene to decide if they wanted to go with him or stay with me though I knew there was a big possibility they would want to be with their dad since they were both going to be angry at me for what I had done. Jake did agree with me, and we had made plans to talk to the kids later that evening before Jake was going to get away by himself for the next few days.

A BROKEN HOME

Weeks had gone by, and I was alone in my house. At least I still had Teddy to keep me company. Andrew and Jolene decided to move with Jake to a condominium, close to the center of town. I had spoken to them only three times since they left, and I had not spoken to Jake at all. The kids were upset with me, and I did not expect otherwise. The days and nights were quiet. It felt lonely and strange to prepare breakfasts and dinners for one. I was fortunate though that Jake and the kids did not want the neighbors to know what really happened other than telling people Jake and I just decided to get a divorce. Most all the neighbors and our closest friends were shocked, well, all but one...Ava. She thought she knew exactly why we did, and she would be right, but I was never going to give her that satisfaction.

It was a stormy evening, I was watching tv in the living room and the doorbell rang. It was detective Bryant. I invited him in as he said he needed to talk to me. Apparently, Doug was scheduled to be released from prison as there was new evidence to prove his innocence. I was so confused. What new evidence? Then who killed Mia? I even pondered for a minute the possibility that Jeff could have been the one who killed Mia, April, and Lauren but only for a minute. Detective Bryant then said he needed to ask me an important question. "Victoria, do you think Jeff and Mia were having an affair?" I shook my head and said "No, that can't be! No!" He said they found a text message on Jeff's phone from back when Mia was still alive. Mia had texted Jeff asking him to meet her at the ravine, the one they would later find her body in. I was at a loss for words. My hands were shaking, and my eyes were welling up. "What are you trying to get at, Detective?" I asked anxiously waiting for his response. "You were the one who told me you saw Mia and Jeff arguing in your house one night and you noticed a bruise on Mia's elbow." "Yes, I did" I continued on, "but Jeff could not have done this, any of this!" Detective Bryant stood up and was getting ready to leave. "Victoria, I know this is difficult for you and I also know you have gone through a lot lately, but I need to focus on the person who has the most against him now, please try to understand that. If Jeff did not have an affair with Mia, at the very least, he must have known her prior to moving across the street." As he walked toward the front door, I grabbed his arm and said, sounding a bit desperate, "I know in my heart Jeff is innocent and I feel bad for Doug having to spend so much time in prison, but Jeff is not your killer." He sighed then said goodnight and I closed the door and went back to watch tv in the living room.
As much as I did not want to, I felt I should call Jake and let him know about Doug being released. But instead, I decided just to text him. He texted back with a response I should have expected from him...WELL, THEN OBVIOUSLY JEFF IS THE GUILTY ONE! I threw my phone down on the sofa, infuriated and sad.

A little later, my daughter texted me and asked if I was okay. I replied to her text by stating I would be fine, apologized and said I loved her and Andrew so much. I did not receive another text from her after that. I knew it would take much more time for her and Andrew to be able to talk to me like they used to before all of this happened. I was more than willing to wait until they were ready rather than pressure them.

As for Andrea, Elizabeth, and Grace, it had been quite a while since I had seen any of them, including Ava. Though I had not been sitting out on my front porch lately since seeing Jeff's motorcycle in his driveway was a constant reminder he was not there, and the neighbors and our friends all seemed to have kept their distance from me since Jake and the kids moved out. I wanted someone to talk to, but I did not know how to approach any of them. What would they think of me if I told them the truth? What were they thinking about Jeff being arrested for three murders? I concluded it would be best for me to just stay away from all of them, at least for now.

I went to grab my mail as it had just been delivered and inside my mailbox was a large envelope addressed to me in pencil with no postage stamp. It must have been placed in the mailbox previously as it clearly did not go through the post office. There was no return address either. I quickly opened it while still standing at the mailbox. There were photos inside. Several of them, some colored, some in black and white. There were pictures of Jeff and I at the beach, Jeff and April in his driveway, Lauren and Jeff at Ava's New Year's Eve party...and one photo of Mia...with Jeff, in the back seat of her SUV. I was stunned by all the photos but even more stunned by the one with Mia. Detective Bryant was right, Jeff and Mia must have had an affair. It all made sense to me now; the way Mia acted that first day Jeff came over to introduce himself and the night I saw them arguing in my house but what about the bruise I noticed on Mia? Was Jeff the person I saw running into and out of Mia's yard? I had so many questions in my head and so many mixed feelings...and I really wanted to know who the envelope was from, so I quickly ran inside to call Detective Bryant.

The next day, I brought the envelope to the police station per Detective Bryant's request. He said he would search the envelope and its contents for fingerprints and would analyze the photos. He was aware of my eagerness to find out where this envelope came from. I did tell him about the man in the car Jeff and I noticed in the parking lot near the beach that day, but I could not remember the make or model.

The weekend came and went. Jake and I had a few short conversations here and there. Both Andrew and Jolene finally stopped by for a couple of hours on Saturday morning, to see Teddy but I was able to get the chance to tell them both I had not planned for any of this to happen, that it just happened, and I needed to make sure they realized that. They both let me know I was still their mother and they still loved me so I took comfort in that, and I knew then that in time, they would be able to forgive me.

Time had gone by, and I had not heard back from Detective Bryant. I was settling into my so-called new life. Jeff was still awaiting his trials and I had not heard from him even though I had written several letters. Life seemed to go on without him and the neighborhood was getting back to some form of normalcy. I still thought about Jeff all the time and I still missed him so very much and then came the phone call from Detective Bryant.

He said he was finally able to find a match to the fingerprints from the envelope of photos I had received in my mailbox. He told me it was someone who worked with my husband but did not want to divulge any more information until he had pieced it all together. I could not believe it and I could not understand why. I wanted to call Jake right away, but Detective Bryant strongly advised me not to as he was still trying to figure out why himself. After being told that, the first thing that came to my mind was Jake must have known about me and Jeff long before he found the letter and he must have had someone following me. But what did that have to do with Mia, April, and Lauren?

UNANSWERED QUESTIONS

I was still waiting for Detective Bryant to update me with more information about the man who sent the photos. Any time I spoke with Jake on the phone, I had to hold myself back from questioning him about it, but I knew I had to let Detective Bryant do his job.

He finally contacted me but would not talk over the phone, so we met for drinks at a bar outside of town. When I arrived, he seemed a bit nervous. I, on the other hand, was extremely nervous. "What is so important that you couldn't tell me over the phone?" I asked. He gently took my hand and began to talk. "Victoria, I am so sorry, but I was wrong about Jeff. I do not believe he is the killer. Your husband is." I abruptly pulled my hand away. "You mean my soon-to-be ex-husband?" "Yes, Jake." He answered. I was in shock. "Why would you ever think...Jake?" I asked in disbelief. He responded, "There is enough evidence to connect him to all three murders from a cell phone we found at the bottom of the ravine...when we checked the phone records, we found many text messages from a cell number belonging to Jake as well as several calls to and from your landline number between he and a man named Peter Whitmore. This man is also a match to the fingerprints we lifted off the photos. Has Jake ever mentioned that name to you before?" He then showed me a photo of the man. "Does this man look familiar to you?" I just sat there in silence for about five minutes. "No, I've never seen him before, and Jake never mentioned anyone named Peter to me...Who is he and why would Jake and this other man want to kill Mia, April, and Lauren?" I continued to sound as if I were defending Jake in some way but that was not my intention, "Jake had never traveled much, and he had always been home early every work night, other than when he worked on side projects." Detective Bryant added, "Peter Whitmore is one of Jake's biggest clients, Jake designs many houses for him throughout the country and I never said Jake killed these women on his own." I took a very deep breath and needed to put my head down for a moment. "Victoria, I know this is a lot to take in, but I need you to listen to me very carefully." I raised my head up, "Sure." "I need you to agree to meet with Jake and discuss your relationship with Jeff." I hesitated. "Ha, what relationship? He's been sitting in jail all this time and I had to find out from you that he had an affair with Mia...He hasn't replied to any of my recent letters...so what relationship do I really have with him now?" Detective Bryant understood where I was coming from but insisted on convincing me to do this.

On my way home, I called Jake and asked him to come by the house the next afternoon so we could

talk. To my surprise he agreed. Then, for the rest of the evening, I thought about Jeff and although I

was upset and angry about the affair he had with Mia, I still loved him...and I wanted him out of jail and with me.

It was the following day, around two in the afternoon and Jake had just arrived at the house. The kids were not with him. We sat at the kitchen table. I was incredibly nervous. He seemed quite jittery as well. I started the conversation by apologizing for what had happened between us. My cell phone was on record per the recommendation of Detective Bryant during our entire conversation. And then it happened. Jake admitted to me that he wanted to see Jeff in prison for the rest of his life since he ruined his. I told him Jeff could not have committed those awful crimes and he agreed and said that it did not matter so long as Jeff rotted in jail. Was it a confession? No, but it was a statement that convinced me and would convince Detective Bryant that Jake knew who did murder Mia, April and Lauren and quite possibly had also been a big part of it. At that point, I was scared and worried about being the next body found in that ravine. I suddenly felt as if I did not know Jake at all anymore. After Jake left, I sent the recording of our conversation to Detective Bryant.

The following afternoon, as I was pulling into my driveway after a visit to the bank, I saw a police cruiser across the street in Jeff's driveway and then there he was! He was just standing there talking with an officer. I, as fast as I could, jumped out of my car and ran across the street yelling his name. I did not even care if any of the neighbors could hear me. "Jeff! Jeff!" The police officer returned to his vehicle and drove away. I ran into Jeff's arms, and he hugged me just as close and tight as I were hugging him. "I missed you so much!" I said, crying. "I missed you just as much if not more!" He replied right before we kissed.

Jeff and I went over to my house, and I made him a home cooked meal as he had not had one in a while. We ate, consumed a bottle of wine, and stayed up until the sunrise, making love, talking, making love again and talking again. It was the best evening of my entire life and it just solidified everything I already knew. I wanted to be with him for the rest of my life.

He was worried about me since I told him about Jake and his connection to the murders. Soon after we left my bed, in the master bedroom not the spare one, I realized I had not had my cell phone with me all night. I then remembered I had left it in my purse which I had left in my car. When I went to grab it, I noticed Detective Bryant had left several voice mails and text messages throughout the evening asking me to call him as soon as I could. I called him back and he told me that the police could not find Peter Whitmore. Now I was getting even more worried because I did not know what would happen next, was I now in danger? Detective Bryant informed me he was going to order police surveillance for both mine and Jeff's houses.

Later that morning, Jeff and I were out on the front porch saying goodbye as he needed to get back home and get some things done. We were kissing for quite a while when Ava walked by with her dog. She just stopped in front of my house and stared at us. I noticed her from the corner of my eye and did not stop kissing Jeff because I did not care if she saw me now. She cleared her throat loud enough so that we would acknowledge her standing there and we did. "Oh, good morning, Ava" I said with a big smile then Jeff said hello. "Well, don't the two of you look extremely happy" she said in sort of a sarcastic tone. Jeff responded, "We are Ava, we really are." Then he said, "it's a beautiful day so you should continue on your walk." She rolled her eyes and off she went.

A NEW BEGINNING OR AN END?

Jeff and I figured the entire neighborhood must have known about us by now since Ava had seen us kissing that morning a couple of weeks ago. We certainly were not hiding anything from anyone as he would continue to go back and forth from his house to mine, though I remained at my house. I did not want to spend time across the street because of Teddy and the kids but Jeff never asked me to go over there anyway. He seemed quite comfortable at my place. It did not matter much to me so long as I could be with him.

It felt refreshing to finally be out together. We would take long motorcycle rides through out town, go out for dinner at restaurants in the center of town, grocery shop at the local market, even go for walks around the neighborhood, all things I used to do with Jake but now I could do with Jeff and not have to worry about the gossip or rumors from the neighbors. It was exhilarating! Andrea and Grace had stopped by recently to let me know they were still my friends, and they were looking forward to getting together with their husbands and Jeff as well. It was comforting to hear them say that because I had felt so alone throughout all of this, and I could now begin to imagine a wonderful future with Jeff.

Soon after Grace and Andrea came by Elizabeth and Dave reached out to both Jeff and I as well. Before long, most of the neighbors and previous friends of Jake and I were reaching out to us. We were both surprised by all the support and acceptance we had finally received by them. We were unsure as to what changed their minds or feelings about us, but we were not going to ask. For the first time I had not felt I had done something so incredibly wrong.

Eventually, Jake found out Jeff was spending most of the nights if not all at the house. He was not too fond of that, but our divorce had just been finalized so there was nothing he could have done about it. I was left the house in the settlement and he controlled the bank accounts. I still did not need to work, and Jeff did pay for most of our date-night expenses.

On my birthday, Jeff surprised me with a weekend getaway at a remote cabin in the woods where he said he had grown up. It was far away, four hours to be exact, but I was excited to see where Jeff grew up and he had not really discussed with me any personal information about his family or upbringing. In fact, we never spoke about any of that. It just never came up. Jake agreed to take Teddy home with him for the weekend and I had informed Detective Bryant of our plans then Jeff and I went on our way.

Once we arrived up at the cabin, Jeff unpacked the car and went into the cabin without me. He came out shortly after and picked me up to carry me into the cabin. It was so romantic, and I knew then just how wonderful the weekend was going to be. When we entered the cabin, I was in awe of how everything was decorated. It was so quaint and comfortable but seemed as if things had been left untouched for quite a while, years even, though it was not dusty at all. Someone must have been looking after the cabin.

It was colder up there than back at home, so Jeff was preparing to light a fire in the fireplace. There were knick-knacks on the mantle but I noticed there were no family pictures and Jeff did tell me this was the cabin he grew up in so I assumed there would have been some family photos displayed somewhere but I did not dwell on it for too long. Jeff was outside chopping firewood and I was putting away the groceries in the kitchen.

We returned from a walk in the woods behind the cabin and it was getting close to dinner time. I decided to start preparing dinner while Jeff was taking a shower. As much as I wanted to join him, we were both famished since we had not eaten all day and I knew there was plenty of time left of the weekend for showering together. I needed a paring knife for the vegetables and instead of bothering Jeff, I started to look in the kitchen drawers, hoping to find one. I had looked through the first three or four drawers without any luck but then I came to a drawer with a broken handle. It seemed to be stuck a bit, so I had to pull hard to get it to open. When I did, I noticed a couple of framed photos in the drawer. I took them out to look at them and I noticed a picture of a young boy who resembled Jeff in a way with his curly dark hair and that adorable smile of his. I then noticed an older man standing next to him, much older than him, an elder age. I heard the bathroom door open, so I quickly shoved the photos back in the drawer and slammed it closed. I had not had the chance to look at the other pictures. When Jeff came into the kitchen he said "Wow, it smells delicious in here Victoria." I replied as he was standing there with nothing, but a towel wrapped around his waist, "Well, you will have to wait. Dinner is simmering and won't be ready for a little while." Jeff then grabbed my hand and pulled me toward the bedroom and said, "Then we have time to make love before dinner." Naturally, I followed his lead.

After dinner, we cuddled on the floor in front of the fire. We had extra-large toss pillows supporting our backs and were finishing the wine from dinner. It was quiet and you could hear crickets outside as we were in the only cabin within miles from the main road. Suddenly, I saw a light come into the window from the front of the cabin. I jumped up and said, "Jeff, where is that light coming from?" He got up right after me and said, "I'm not sure, let me go look." He made his way to the front door and opened it only to see a car quickly backing out of the driveway. It was very dark, neither of us could really see the car, only the headlights. I asked Jeff genuinely concerned, "Aren't we the only ones up here for miles?" He put his arms around me, kissed my cheek and replied, "Yes honey, we are. It was probably just someone who was lost." We then decided to go off to bed and though, I was still feeling uneasy about the car, I was looking forward to Jeff making love to me again. The next morning, Jeff and I went out for another walk around the cabin. It was cold out but much warmer directly in the sun, we came to a small brook and sat on a large rock for a while just talking. He began to tell me things about his childhood, memories he had of the brook we were at. I did not ask questions for I just loved sitting there and listening to his stories. He did eventually tell me the cabin belonged to his grandfather, who had raised him since he was a little boy. He seemed a bit sad when he talked about him, but he never did say what happened to him. He never even told me his grandfather's name.

When we returned to the cabin, Jeff needed to chop more wood for the fireplace. I needed to get lunch ready. As I was in the kitchen, I remembered the pictures I had found. I knew Jeff would be outside for a while, so I decided to take the pictures out again. I had already seen the one with whom I assumed was both Jeff and his grandfather but then I looked at another photo and could not believe what I was looking at. It was a photo of a man standing on the front steps of the house across the street, Jeff's house. It looked better kept than now and was an unusual color when the photo had been taken but I was sure it was the same house. I did not know what I should l do, or what I should ask or say to Jeff, but at that moment, I just wanted to get out of there and go back home. With all that I had dealt with already, I did not want to be told any more lies. I wanted so badly to contact Detective Bryant, but there wasn't any cell service. After taking several deep breaths, I forced myself to calm down and convinced myself that Jeff would not intentionally lie to me and there must be a good explanation as to why he never told me about the house across the street. Why he never said his family had once owned the house before he moved in. Why he acted as if he was new to the neighborhood when he moved in. I had so many doubts now and I wanted answers to so many questions.
When Jeff came back in, he could tell I was frazzled. He asked what was wrong and I told him I suddenly was not feeling well. He walked me to into the bedroom and after I laid down on the bed, he covered me with a blanket and told me to get some rest and he would make dinner for us later. He was being extremely sweet and caring.

When I woke up from my nap, I could hear pots and pans rattling because Jeff was in the kitchen cooking dinner. "Well, how did you sleep, honey?" He asked as he gave me a quick kiss before going back to what he was doing. "Um, I slept fine." I did not want to say what I said next, but I did. "Um...Jeff...I found some old pictures yesterday in that drawer over there with the broken handle." He put down the towel he had been wiping his hands with. "What pictures?" he asked. I then walked over to the drawer and opened it only to notice they were no longer there. "They were right in here!" I said in a loud tone, "where did they go Jeff?" He came over to me and slammed the door shut. "They are old photos that mean nothing to me!" At that time, I knew I had made Jeff angry and upset with me and I did not want him to be.

That evening, we again sat by the fire while cuddling under a blanket. I knew then Jeff had such a hold on me. I loved him that much I could not find any faults with him. He was secretive and reserved at times but those were a couple of reasons why I was so mesmerized by him. We ended up in bed much earlier than the evening before. We made love for most of the rest of the night as we knew our romantic weekend away was coming to an end and we needed to leave early in the morning.

When I was in the bedroom packing what little items I had brought with me, I went into the closet to look for a laundry bag of some sort. I then came across a woman's scarf up on a shelve. I pulled it down and I noticed a monogram stitched on one of the ends, the letters MDA. It took me a minute but then I realized it must have stood for Mia Ann Defoe. I gasped loudly as I placed my hand over my mouth. I had been allowing so many questions to be unanswered by Jeff, I could not let this one go. I walked out of the bedroom and while holding the scarf in my hand, I confronted Jeff in the living room. "What is this? Who is this? Jeff, did this belong to Mia?" I had not given him a chance to answer as I just kept pressing him with questions, "Why do you have this? Did you have an affair with Mia?" He stood there a few feet away from me and put his head down for a moment. "Victoria, please, come sit down next to me and I will explain everything to you." He was calm, I not so much but I did agree to sit beside him, and we talked and talked and talked. I could sense he was being completely honest with me. He confessed he and Mia did have an affair which began months before he moved into the house across the street. Detective Bryant was right. They had met at a bar outside of town one evening when Mia was out with some friends from her college days, but that the affair had ended a short time later and long before she was found dead. He assured me he had nothing to do with her death. He also told me he and Mia had both been receiving items such as photos of the two of them together in the mail for some time and that he was trying to convince her to go to the police as he was worried about her safety, but she refused and that is why they appeared to be having an argument at my house that night of the barbecue. It all began to make sense.

He also made me aware there were still many things I did not know about him, or Jake, but he would not tell me because he would then fear for my safety as well. Although, he did give the inclination that it had all involved fraudulent business dealings with Doug's company which Jeff had been the main investor for and to my surprise, Jake and Peter Whitmore were also prime investors in the company. But when I asked Jeff what all that had to do with the murders of Mia, April, and Lauren, he said that Jake and Peter were involved to aid in destroying everything Jeff had in his life because of the considerable amount of money at stake. I contemplated telling Detective Bryant when I got back home everything I had been told by Jeff, but I knew if I did, Jeff would still face criminal charges for embezzlement and fraud. Jeff said he could never go to jail again and he would do whatever he needed to, to ensure that did not happen. I felt helpless as I told him there was nothing I could do to help him. He told me how much he loved me, and he wanted me to be safe. It was getting later in the day, and we knew we had a long four-hour drive ahead of us, so we packed up the car and went on our way back home. There were a lot of moments of silence during the ride home and some small conversations, but we did not speak about our discussion at the cabin.

When we arrived in my driveway, Jeff grabbed our things from the trunk. He placed my bags on my front porch and carried his across the street. When he reached the top of his driveway, he dropped his bags and ran back over to me. He hugged me tighter than usual and whispered in my ear, "I love you." I then went into my house, planning to see him again the following day.

ESCAPE

It was the middle of the night, and I was woken by the sound of sirens and bright flashes of red and blue lights coming from outside. I jumped out of bed and ran to the front window to see what was happening and I saw Jeff's house engulfed in flames. I threw on my robe, quickly ran out of my house yelling Jeff's name extremely loud and began running across the street. Detective Bryant stopped me in the middle of the street. As he was holding me back, I was screaming the word "No!" over and over while crying uncontrollably. Detective Bryant told me there was nothing anyone could do and as he continued to restrain me, I just watched the entire house burn down to the ground.

The next morning, I went out to get the mail. I could see smoke still coming from the ground where Jeff's house once stood. There was a strong smoke odor within the neighborhood which was sure to linger for days. I noticed lying in the back of the mailbox, a piece of white paper folded in half. I opened it. It was a note that read:

Dear Victoria,
Please forgive me!
Jeff
Xo

I held the note up close to my heart and cried. I wanted so much at that moment to touch Jeff again.

A couple of weeks after the fire, Detective Bryant called to inform me the arson investigators confirmed the fire was set intentionally and that it had started in the basement. He also wanted me to know there was no evidence that Jeff died in the fire. He did, however, state there were remains of a body found in the basement and that those remains belonged to a man named Edward James Stevens, Jeff's grandfather. I had never told the Detective about the photos I found up in the cabin nor did I ever tell him about the note from Jeff I found in my mailbox.

Three months had gone by, and I had not seen nor heard from Detective Bryant. I figured he had been preoccupied with another case. It was a beautiful, sunny day, a little breezy though very warm. A developer had purchased the now empty lot across the street and building was getting under way. I had just returned from getting a coffee in town and as I was getting out of my car, Detective Bryant had pulled up to my driveway. He got of his car and while holding my coffee in one hand and my keys and purse in the other, I said "Detective Bryant, I didn't think I would see you again." He walked further up the driveway towards me. "Please, call me Shawn. I just wanted to stop by to check on you." "That's sweet," I responded then went ahead to ask, "Would you like to come in for a cup of coffee? I grabbed one in town, but I don't mind making a fresh pot." He politely thanked me for the offer but said he needed to get back to the precinct and we looked into each other's eyes for a couple of minutes. "Victoria are you okay?" he asked sounding genuinely concerned. "I replied, "I will be." He then took a few steps closer to me while saying, "I would love to take you out for dinner sometime." I paused briefly before responding, "I would like that...someday." "Well," he said as he stood right in front of me, using his hands to gently move my hair away from my face, "until then," and he leaned in to kiss me. I did not push him away. In fact, I kissed him back. It was nice and I felt safe.

After the kiss, he walked back to his car. Before getting in, he turned around and said, "I hope you can begin a new chapter in your life," and he smiled. I stood there nodding my head then replied, "When I do, I hope it includes you," and I smiled back.

When he drove away, we both knew we would be seeing each other again.

A NEW VISION

A year later, things around the neighborhood seem to be back to normal, as normal as they can be considering all that has happened. With all that has changed, there is still so much that has stayed the same. There has been a new house built across the street, though the old one is gone, the memories are not. It is a beautiful colonial style home, enormous in size, with a three-car garage. Ava no longer has the biggest house in the neighborhood. A FOR SALE sign has recently been placed on the front lawn.

Andrew and Jolene are finally back home with me. Andrew graduated from college and is on the hunt for a full-time job. Jolene decided to take a year off from college to "find herself" and with everything that happened between her dad and I, I agreed it was a good idea for her to do so. Jake and Peter are both serving time for being accessories to the murders. Doug was back in prison not for murder but on conspiracy charges. The police had never found the man who killed Mia, April, and Lauren and Jake, Peter and Doug all knew he would never be found, and I often wonder if I could be next.

As for Detective Bryant, now Captain Bryant, well Shawn, he and I have been dating for over six months now. He gets along well with Andrew and Jolene, and they do like him. It has been nice having a father-figure around for them. Our relationship is not too serious, but I can see things eventually going that way.

Every now and then I receive a phone call on my cell from an unknown number but when I answer, I can only hear a faint breathing sound in the background...and I often wonder if it is Jeff.

CLARITY

I could feel a warm, clenching sensation in my hand while at the same time, a soft, gentle stroke on my cheek. My eyes were blinking uncontrollably trying to focus. Everything was blurry but I could see dark shadows near me. I could hear muffled voices in the distance. I inhaled and exhaled as if I were taking my first breath. I slowly moved my head from side to side and then saw a man next to me with his head resting on my arm. I mumbled in an incredibly soft whisper, "Jeff?" "Vicky!" he said excitingly as he raised his head, "you're awake!" I still had not gotten my bearings yet, still did not have sharp vision. I looked up to see bright lights on the ceiling. I was surrounded by machines and monitors and attached to all sorts of tubing and wires. I then closed my eyes for a moment. The man leaned over me and kissed my forehead, "I'm here and you're going to be okay." I opened my eyes and looked up at him, "Jake... where am I?" I asked with a frightened, shaky voice. He answered while holding my hand, "You are in the hospital. You have been in a coma for the past six months. I have been here right by your side, honey." It took a bit for me to take in what I was just told. My head hurt terribly, and I could not move my arms much or my legs at all. "What happened?" I asked, feeling uneasy. He then replied, "there was an accident...a terrible accident." I raised my head as high as I could and frantically asked, "Where are Andrew and Jolene?" He responded in a reassuring tone, "They are both fine, they weren't in the accident, they will be here soon." I replied with a big sigh of relief. Then a doctor entered the room. "Well, Vicky, I am very glad to see you're awake." He came over to my bed. "You have been asleep for quite a while, six months to be exact." He continued, "I'm Dr. Millis. You have been through a severe trauma, but you will be okay. I have ordered several tests for the next few days but until then, I want you to get plenty of rest so we can get you on your feet again and back home with your family where you belong." He had a good bedside manner. Jake stood up and shook his hand, "Thank you Dr. Millis." The doctor then turned to me with a smile before leaving the room.

Jake returned to my side and held my hand again. He kissed my cheek and said, "Oh, Vicky, I thought I lost you," as he wiped a tear from his eye. I then asked, "What kind of accident was I in?" He waited a minute before responding. "You don't remember?" I took a few minutes to think but nothing came to mind. "No, I don't remember anything." Then something did come to mind. "Wait...I do remember an officer helping me." "Yes, that was Detective Bryant. He was the one who found you." I was confused even more. "Found me where?" I asked. He answered, "In the ravine...the car slid off the road and into the ravine." I took a deep breath as Jake continued to tell me the details of what had happened. "You were coming back with the girls from Lauren's bachelorette party- "He then stopped and said, "maybe we should talk about this later...the doctor said you need to get some rest." "No!" I said abruptly. "I need to know what happened; you need to tell me what happened!" Jake then laid his arms on the side of my bed and folded his hands." He looked at me then put his head down, "Honey, you were the only survivor...Mia, April and Lauren didn't make it." I turned away and started to cry which then turned into uncontrollable sobbing. I could not speak. Jake held me and said as he too was crying, "It wasn't your fault...it was not your fault." I turned back to him, and he held my hand up to his face. "We will get through this, I promise." He wiped the tears from my face, and we just stared at each other for a while. "I need you Jake, please don't ever leave me...I love you so much." He kissed me on the lips and replied, "I will be with you for the rest of our lives."
Later, Andrew and Jolene came to the hospital. I was so happy to see them, and they were just as happy to see me. They sat with me and talked about what they were up to the last six months. After a while, Jake suggested the three of them leave so that I could get some rest.

The next morning, Jake arrived at the hospital early. It was not long after he showed up when the nurse came to get me for testing. I was gone for about three hours and when I returned to my room, Jake was still there, lying in a chair, asleep. I was still in my wheelchair and told the nurse to leave me in it and she pushed me next to him. I just wanted to sit there and watch him sleep. I knew he must have been exhausted.

When he woke, I said "Jake, you didn't have to stay here. You really need to get some rest yourself." As soon as he was about to say something, a man in a suit with a police badge on his jacket walked into the room. Jake abruptly got up and walked over to the man. "Detective Bryant...what are you doing here?" The detective responded, "I wanted to check in with you and see how your wife was. I stopped by the house and your son Andrew said you'd be here." Jake wheeled me over to him. "This is my wife Vicky" I cut him off in mid-sentence and said, "I prefer to be called Victoria." "Well, Victoria," the detective continued, "I am deeply sorry about the accident, you are lucky to be alive." I thanked him and put my head down. He then went ahead to say, "We have not yet determined the cause of the accident, and we may never." Jake asked the detective, "Do you believe it was an accident?" He answered, "I'm not sure." I started to cry, and Jake put his arms around me. At that moment, I screamed, "It's my fault! It's all my fault!" Detective Bryant calmly said to me, "You were not at fault, all your toxicology reports were clear of any drugs or alcohol. We have determined speed was not a factor. We even checked your cell phone for calls and text messages made within the time of the accident and found none since the time you would have left the restaurant." He paused for a moment and continued. "Look, we did match skid marks to your tires for quite a distance before you went off the road and into the ravine." He again paused a moment, "If there is any latest information, I will let you know." He said he was sorry, handed me his card and told Jake and I to call him if we needed anything. As he was walking away, I asked him, "Do you think they suffered?" He turned to me and replied, "April died on the way to the hospital, Mia passed away during surgery and... Lauren was dead at the scene; she was the only one not wearing her seatbelt." I put my hand on my forehead and cried. I then said, "Detective Bryant, I remember you...you saved my life." He put his head down for a minute then said, "I only wish I were on that road sooner then maybe it never would have happened." We both just looked at one another for a moment then he walked out of the room. After he left, I looked at Jake and said, "Please get the nurse, I want to lie back in bed," and I continued to cry.

Just as the nurse was walking out of the room, Dr. Millis walked in and closed the door behind him. I could tell by the look on his face he did not have good news. "How are feeling Vicky?" he asked in a concerned tone. I responded, "I have a bit of a headache but otherwise I feel okay." He then walked over to the bottom of my bed and began to touch my feet. As he was moving them back and forth, he asked "Can you feel this?" I did not answer him for a few minutes. I could see what he was doing to my feet, but I could not feel it. "Um, no...no, I can't feel anything." I turned to look at Jake as my eyes were welling up. "Jake," I said sadly. He took my hand and asked "Doctor, what does this mean?" Dr. Millis responded as he was looking at my chart, "I received some of the results from the testing you had done earlier," he paused for a minute, "you have a considerable amount of damage to your spine." He cleared his throat then continued, "because of this, it will take a long time and a lot of effort on your part to be able to get up and walk again," he again cleared his throat, "and there is a chance you will never walk again." I took a deep breath and put my head down. Jake was rubbing my shoulder. Then Dr. Millis continued to speak. "Vicky, I would like to transfer you to a rehabilitation center so you can begin treatment immediately." I was quick to respond. "Absolutely not! I want to go home...I need to get back home." Jake then intervened. "Can't she do outpatient treatment?" Dr. Millis gave a look of disagreement but then answered, "She can.... but Vicky, you must understand if you do not receive the proper and consistent treatment, you will end up in a wheelchair for the rest of your life." I gave a heavy sigh and said, "I understand." I then wanted to mention something to him. "Why can't I remember things?" He replied, "Well, you suffered a serious brain injury due to the accident." He continued, "it's common for someone to forget a period prior to and during such a traumatic event. You may remember your husband, children, certain things during the accident but you may, not even realizing it, be blocking out painful memories of the past. It will take time, but you will eventually begin to remember bits and pieces of certain things though you may never fully regain your memory...I would recommend seeing a therapist when you feel up to it. You've been through a lot." I responded with a thank you, then he said, "I would like to keep you here for at least the next few days to monitor your progress and conduct some more tests, but I will get you out of here and back home soon." He then added, "I promise." I nodded my head and said as he was opening the door to leave, "Dr. Millis, please call me Victoria." He smiled and walked away. I then looked at Jake and said, "Please go home Jake...I will be fine...I just want to be alone now." He seemed a little upset but then replied, "Ok, I will be back in the morning...I Love you." I watched him walk out of the room and I just broke down and cried but eventually I fell asleep.

I spent the next few days in the hospital and other than not being able to walk, I felt better. My headaches did not seem as painful as they were, though I still could not remember much before the accident and absolutely nothing during the accident other than Detective Bryant.

COMING TO TERMS

The day to go home had finally arrived. I was excited but also scared. I could not wait to see Teddy again. I could not imagine how much that little dog must have missed me. There was so much I could not remember before the accident yet there were many things I thought I remembered but were not true. As Jake and I were driving home, we were talking about the neighborhood. I asked him, "Hey, did anyone ever buy the house across the street?" He quickly glanced at me then continued to keep his eyes on the road. "What house?" I replied, "The one that was built after the fire." He shook his head a little and responded, "Honey, we built our house on a lot that a house once stood before it was burned down." I was confused. "Oh," I said and then I was silent for the rest of the drive.

When we arrived home, Andrew and Jolene were waiting for us in the driveway. Jake helped me out of the car and into my wheelchair. As he was pushing me toward the front door, I turned my head around to look across the street. "Wait!" I said loudly, "turn the wheelchair around." He responded, "I think we should just head into the house." I yelled in a bit of an angry tone, "Jake, please!" He turned me around and I was now facing the house across the street. I just stared at it for a moment. Jake then asked, "Honey, are you alright?" I paused for a minute as my eyes began to water, "I don't know," I said quietly, "I really don't know." He leaned over and gave me a kiss while saying, "I love you...let's go in the house."

When I entered the house, it felt strange. It did not feel like my house. It did not feel like my home. There were framed family photos of me, Jake, and the kids everywhere. This was my home, but I did not feel right being in it. I wheeled myself over to the largest window in the living room which faced the front of the house. I could not stop staring at the house across the street. Jake came into the room with a cup of hot tea for me and pulled over a chair to sit next to me. "What are you looking at?" he asked. He then pulled down the blinds of the window. I answered him when I finished taking a sip of my tea. "I can't remember things." He replied while holding my hand, "Honey, you heard what Dr. Millis said. It is going to take time and right now, all you need to remember are me and the kids and how much we love you...how much I love you...and that we're a family." Just as he gave me a kiss, the doorbell rang. Jolene had run to answer it. "Mom!" she yelled as she was carrying a large flower arrangement into the room, "these are for you!" "They're beautiful," I commented, "who are they from?" She then opened the attached card and read the message. "Please get well soon, Doug." She then continued to say, "that was very nice of Mia's husband to send you flowers." I started to cry and replied, "Yes, it was." I remembered Doug.

A week went by, and I was beginning to remember little things here and there. Jake and the kids were being extremely helpful. They were all helping with the laundry, errands, cooking and keeping the house neat and tidy. Jake was very attentive to my needs. He was back at work full-time but had stopped scheduling side work on evenings and weekends. Andrew and Jolene would bicker with each other occasionally, due to being home together so much, but Teddy stayed by my side and kept me calm.

I had my first session of physical therapy. Jake took the day off from work and brought me to the rehab center. He waited in the car for me until I was finished. It was difficult. I never realized how hard it would be to move my legs when I cannot feel them move. On our way home, I asked Jake to stop at the ravine. He did not think that was a good idea, but I told him I needed to go there to say goodbye to Mia, April, and Lauren. When we arrived at the ravine, he carried me to a nearby rock and sat me down. He stood behind me and I just stared down at the ravine and cried. I could not believe Detective Bryant found me...well, us. There were still skid marks on the ground from my car just as the detective said. While saying a prayer for each of them, I apologized, though I knew it was not my fault, but I was the one driving. Maybe if one of them were driving, they would have been able to control the car better than I did. Maybe if I were not the one driving, we would have taken a different route home. Maybe if I were not the one...well, I could think about the 'what ifs' for hours. Jake held me and asked, "Honey, are you ready to go now?" I wiped the tears from my face and answered, "Yes, I am." He picked me up and carried me back to the car. On our way home, I thanked him for bringing me to the ravine. He responded by telling me he would bring me back there whenever I wanted him to.
Another week had gone by. I was sitting out on my front walkway with a cup of coffee and Teddy by my side, as usual. It was a beautiful morning. The kids went to do grocery shopping for me, and Jake was at work, but I felt comfortable being left alone, for a little while anyway. Then a van came down the driveway, it was the local florist. The man parked and came out of the van holding an enormous bouquet of flowers. As he was approaching me, he asked, "Are you Victoria Hammond?" I answered right away, "Yes, I am." He handed the flowers to me and said, "Have a wonderful day." The bouquet was absolutely stunning with roses and a variety of flowers in all different shades of yellow. I searched for a card though one was not attached.

Soon after the flower delivery, the kids got back from shopping. Jolene got out of the car and rushed over to me as Andrew was unloading the groceries. "Mom, those flowers are gorgeous!" she said. "Yes, they are." I replied. She then asked, "Are they from Dad?" I paused a minute before answering, "I guess they are." She wheeled me back in the house and into the living room. She and Andrew helped me on the sofa, and I started to watch a movie on tv while the kids were putting away the groceries. Jolene had put the flowers in a vase and placed them on the kitchen island. Andrew then left to go out with friends and Jolene was about to leave also when Jake walked in. I heard them talking in the kitchen. Jolene said to him, "Hey Dad, the flowers you sent Mom are beautiful." Jake asked her, "What flowers?" She replied, "These ones...in her favorite color." Jake did not say anything for a minute then said, "Oh, yes, I hope she likes them." As soon as I heard him say that I yelled out to the kitchen, "Yes Jake, I love them!"

Jolene came in to give me a kiss before she went out and then Jake walked in. He came over to me to reposition my pillow behind me so I would be more comfortable. He then sat in the chair next to me. I looked at him and said, "Thank you for the flowers, you didn't have to send them to me." He put his head down without saying a word. "Jake," I asked, "what's wrong?" He looked up at me and his eyes were watery. I knew what I needed to ask next. "The flowers weren't from you, were they?" He stood up and said, "I can't do this with you right now." I asked, "Do what? What can't you do?" He replied, "Vicky, not now," as he walked out of the room. I yelled, "You know I prefer to be called Victoria!" He quickly turned around and yelled back, "That's what he used to call you!" I did not understand what he had just said. He then walked back into the room, and I could see how angry he was. "I cannot stand watching you sit in front of the window and stare at the house across the street!" I looked at him as calm as I could be and said, "Jake, please, help me understand what you're talking about." He sighed heavily, "Jeff lives across the street!" as he continued to yell at me. "Do you remember now?!" Just then, I remembered waking up in the hospital and faintly whispering the name 'Jeff.' I then had to ask, "Why does that matter?" Jake responded even angrier, "Because you were in love with him!" and he stormed out of the room. I said frantically, "Jake, please don't go...talk to me!" He did not say anything back and left the house while slamming the door behind him.

At that moment, my head began to ache. I was trying desperately to remember why Jake would be so angry and upset. I was now left alone in the house and had never felt so alone in my life. I wanted so much to be able to call Mia, but she was gone. So, instead I turned off the tv and cried myself to sleep. A couple of hours later, Jake came home. The kids were still out. He came into the living room and turned on the light as it was dark. I woke up and we stared at each other for a few minutes, and I said, "Jake, I am so sorry I hurt you." He walked over to me and sat on the sofa next to me. He grabbed my hand and while holding it gently said, "It took me a while to forgive you and forget...and now I am scared you will remember... and you'll want to be with him again." I took a while to respond as I tried to remember. "Jake...I am your wife, the mother of Andrew and Jolene..." I then put my other hand over his, "and I don't want to be anywhere else." I leaned in to kiss him. He kissed me back and we cried together for a couple of minutes. As for the flowers, Jake threw them in the trash, and we never spoke of them again. Although, we both knew they must have been from Jeff. At that time, I did not press Jake to tell me anything more as I did not want him to further upset him. Both of us agreed to never mention Jeff's name again.

RECONNECTED

Jake and both kids were at work. It was a hot, sunny afternoon and I had not been out for a while. The mail had just been delivered so I decided to walk out to the mailbox and grab it. It took me a bit to get there as I was still not completely used to my walker yet. As I was walking back to the house, I heard someone call my name. "Victoria!" I turned around and it was him. It was Jeff. I turned back around because I did not know what to do or say and I continued walking back to the house. He then yelled, "Victoria! Wait!" I stopped again and looked back to see him running across the street and into my driveway towards me. When he approached me, I turned my body around to face him. He said to me in a soft voice, "Hey," as we gazed into each other's eyes for a moment, "I've missed you so much." Then he asked with a concerned tone, "Are you okay?" I ignored his first statement but answered his question, "I'll be fine...I'm getting better every day." He responded with a smile, "I'm glad," he paused for a minute, "I thought I had lost you." I immediately replied, "You should go...Jake will be home from work soon." He grabbed my arms but gently, "Victoria...don't be like this...not after everything we've been through." I then anxiously replied, "Please let go of me...I don't remember things, I don't remember the accident," I looked right at him and continued to say, "I don't remember us." I turned around and began to walk away and as he stopped me, he said, "We were in love." I put my head down and paused for a minute. "I broke it off with you, I ended it." He nodded his head a bit and asked, "Is that what Jake told you?" I did not say anything, and he continued. "You were going to leave him, and I was calling off the wedding...but then the accident happened." "I can't," I began to cry a little, "I can't deal with this right now." He came closer to me and put his hand on my cheek and said, "I still love you...and I know you'll still love me when you can remember." He looked at me intensely and then asked, "You really don't remember, do you?" I took a minute before answering him. "No, I remember some things but not..." and I paused again, "...not us and not the accident or what caused the accident." He then wiped the tears from my face and said, "I know when you all left the restaurant that night, you and Lauren were arguing." "Arguing?" I asked confused. "About what?" He sighed then replied, "You left your cell phone on the table at the restaurant and Lauren went back in to get it for you while the three of you waited in the car..." he sighed again, "she read the last text message I sent to you that evening." He continued, "it said I was going to call off the wedding so you and I could be together." I was in shock. "What?!" I took a deep breath. Jeff went on to say, "She then looked through your phone at all the other messages that you and I texted to each other...Victoria, she was devastated and angry at both of us and apparently when she returned to your car, well, things just blew up between the two of you." I put my hand on my forehead. "How do you even know any of this? Were you there?" "No, of course I wasn't there," he answered, then continued to say, "Lauren called me from your phone before she went back to your car.... and April texted me during the ride home...she told me Lauren was screaming at you and shoving your phone in your face." I started shaking, "Oh my god! It was all my fault!" He put his hand on my shoulder, "No, it wasn't! It was just a tragic accident." His eyes started to well up and he said, "Victoria, I lost both a sister and a soon to be ex-fiancé that night, along with our friend, Mia...but when I got the call from Detective Bryant, I could not help but immediately ask him if you survived." There was a lull of silence. "I'm sorry Jeff, for your losses...but I cannot go back." I looked away for a moment to think about what I was going to say next then turned back to him and said, "I need to stay with Jake...I need to be with my family." He said nothing. He just stared at me with a sad look on his face then he leaned in to kiss me...and we kissed...and it triggered something for me. I remembered that kiss and that is when I felt like I was really missing something, or I should say, someone." After several seconds, I pulled away from him while saying, "I can't do this," and started to walk back to the house. He then said, "I hope you liked the flowers...I know yellow is your favorite color." I stopped for a second but then continued to walk into the house. Jeff went back across the street, and I went into my living room to sit in front of the window. After a little while, I saw Jake pull into the driveway. I moved away from the window quickly and walked into the kitchen. I had no intention of telling him about Jeff coming by earlier.

It had been a couple of months since I left the hospital. My physical therapy was progressing quite nicely. I was now able to get up and walk around using a cane but still a walker at times to improve my balance. I had started seeing a therapist to help with my memory loss. I had not been sleeping well since I saw Jeff that day. I had been having severe headaches, nightmares about the accident and dreams about Jeff but still could not decipher between my imagination and reality. I had not seen Jeff since that day, but I wanted to...I just did not know how. My therapist said I was self-consciously blocking out memories to avoid feelings of guilt. She was optimistic about me regaining my full memory in time, but I was not too sure if I even wanted to.

REMEMBERING

It was a very warm Sunday morning and Jake was up early doing yard work. Andrew was working a double shift and Jolene had spent the night before at a friend's house and would not be home until dinner time. I was sitting out on the front lawn soaking up the sun. It is much shadier in the back yard. Jake had just finished mowing the back lawn and was coming around to mow the front. I noticed Jeff across the street, sitting on his front porch, just staring over at me. I could not help but stare back at him, while also trying to keep Jake in view from the corner of my eye. I had been remembering a few things about Jeff and me but did not let on to Jake that I had. I remembered being across the street, several mornings, after Jake and the kids would leave the house. I remembered a particular wine I would drink with Jeff, and I also remembered how it felt when he held me. The memories were coming back but I did not know what to do with them. Do I just forget about them? Do I tell Jake I am starting to recall the past or do I just leave the memories in the past and focus on building new ones with Jake...or with Jeff? I was becoming even more confused than I was when I woke up from the coma. Just as I was contemplating the scenarios in my mind, Jeff was heading down our driveway. I suddenly became excited and nervous at the same time. I said to myself, what he is doing here? Jake noticed him right away and quickly shut off the lawn mower. From a distance, Jake asked him, "What are you doing here?" in a not so friendly voice. Jeff answered with hesitation, "Um...I just wanted to apologize Jake...for everything that happened." I could tell by the look on Jake's face, he really wanted to punch Jeff but that was not who Jake was. Jake avoided conflict whenever he could, which was one of the biggest reasons why I loved him...but to see Jeff stand there in front us like that was, well, it made me really feel differently about him. It made me realize why I would have fallen in love with him and at that moment, I felt as if I still were. Not much was said after Jeff's apology. Jake went back to mowing the lawn and I went back into the house. Jeff had gone back across the street.

Later that evening, after dinner, Jake poured me a glass of wine and we sat out on the back patio. He lit a fire and it felt as if nothing had changed between us though so much had. We talked about his work for a bit then about my rehab and therapy. There were periods of silence when neither of us would say anything. I knew I needed to get answers to some questions I had so I suddenly asked him, "When did you know? How did you find out?" He knew exactly what I was talking about. He took a while to answer me. "One afternoon, I had to come back home during lunch to grab some paperwork..." he took a sip of his wine, then continued, "I was driving down the street and saw you coming out of Jeff's house...I turned around quickly and went back to work. I asked him, "Why didn't you say anything to me about it?" He responded, "What would your excuse had been?" I knew I would not have had one. "I don't know what I would have said." He then said to me, "Later that night, when you were asleep, I looked through your phone and read the text messages between the two of you." I said to myself, first Jake, then Lauren, who else looked through my phone? I finished my glass of wine with a large sip as I did not know how to respond to what he had just told me. "I knew you were having an affair and I knew it had been going for a while," he put his head down for a minute then looked back up at me, "so I turned to Mia." I was stunned by his comment. "What do you mean, you turned to Mia? Mia knew?" I asked impatiently waiting for him to answer. "She only knew because I told her." I was now becoming a little angry at him. "You involved Mia, my best friend! My – "He then interrupted me to say, "We were involved." "Wait!" I said, "what do you mean involved?" He put down his wine glass as I refilled mine. "I was so distraught over your affair with Jeff, Mia and I spent a lot of time talking to each other...the nights I had told you I was working late, well, I was with her." I stood up and threw my glass on the ground it shattered as I was yelling at him. "How could you Jake?! How could you make me feel so guilty all this time for hurting you?!" He stood up and placed his hand on my shoulder while asking me to sit back down. I sat down and he poured more wine into his glass. "Two wrongs don't make a right," he said, "I know that, but it didn't last long with Mia and I...we weren't serious, it was something different. I just needed someone to vent to." He sighed a moment, "it wasn't anything like what you had with Jeff." I took a sip of wine then nodded my head back and forth a couple times and asked, "Why did you tell me I ended the affair?" He looked a little confused. "Don't you remember doing that?" Then I got mad. "No Jake, I don't remember doing that because I didn't do that! You lied to me!" He then stood back up and asked with an agitated tone, "Are you speaking with him again?" I looked up at him and answered, "I have...but not for the past couple of months." He then grabbed the empty bottle of wine, ready to leave and said, "Maybe we can't get through this." I responded, "Maybe we can't... but you're the one who's not being honest ...I'm the one who can't remember everything." As he walked away, he told me to be careful of the broken glass and that he would clean it up later.

The next few months were quiet though neither of us wanted the kids to sense anything was wrong. We had our regular family dinners at the table together and functioned as normally. I no longer needed the use of the cane, my headaches had subsided, and I had regained most of my memory, other than the night of the accident. I still went to the rehab center once a week and saw my therapist every two weeks. I remembered when the affair with Jeff began, some of the details were still a little foggy but I could remember the important things...and most of the good things. I had not seen or heard from Jeff at all since that day he came to apologize to Jake. I missed him terribly, but I was not ready to go to him yet. Jake and I had so much we needed to discuss. Andrew had accepted a job offer in another state and Jolene had made the decision to go to college. We had many things to prepare for aside from filing for divorce which we both agreed had to be done at some point.

A DOUBLE LIFE?

Andrew was all settled into his apartment a few states away and had started his new job. Jolene had moved into her dorm at a college outside of town, only about thirty minutes away. Jake and I attended our first meeting to begin the divorce proceedings. We decided to use the same attorney to make things quicker and easier. We knew it would be a civil divorce with no hard feelings on either side. I was now prepared to go to Jeff and tell him how much I had missed him and to let him know I was finally ready to begin our new life together.

It was a Saturday morning. Jake had to go into work for a meeting. As soon as he left, I got ready to go across the street. As I was walking over, I noticed a woman putting a FOR SALE sign on Jeff's front lawn. I immediately approached her, "Excuse me." She turned around. "May I help you?" I took a second before responding, "Um, yes...this house is for sale?" She replied, "It is, are you interested?" I just stood there for a moment then said, "No, no, I'm not...Um...I was actually looking to speak with the homeowner." She responded, "Oh, he already moved out. The house is being sold furnished." I gasped for a breath as I could not believe what I had just heard. I then eagerly searched through my phone for a photo of Jeff. When I found one, I showed it to the woman. "Um, is this the homeowner?" She only needed a second to answer. "Yes, that's Mr. Sterling." I paused a minute. "Mr. Sterling?" I asked. She replied, "Yes, his first name is Joe...but he no longer owns this house, the realtor I work for purchased it about a month ago." She continued to say, "Apparently, Mr. Sterling was in a rush to sell." At that moment, I almost fell to the ground, and I walked back across the street as fast as my legs would let me. When I got back into my house, I texted Jeff and within seconds, I received an error message stating the text did not go through so then I decided to call his number and it was out of service. I began sobbing and felt as if I could not breath. My heart felt like it broke inside of me. I could not understand what was happening. Where was Jeff? Why did he just up and leave? Was he really Jeff Stevens or was he Joe Sterling? Nothing made sense...none of it made any sense. Once I stopped crying, I then became angry. Why would he leave me like this? He was supposed to wait for me. He said he loved me...but then I realized, I was angrier at myself for not running to him sooner. I took for granted that he would wait for me until I was ready to move on with him, but he could not wait any longer...and now it was too late for us.

MOVING ON

Much time had passed, and life went on. Jake had bought a small house for him and his girlfriend, Helen, whom he met shortly after he and I divorced, near the center of town and I remained in what was once our home. Andrew would call me once a week, usually on Sunday mornings and Jolene and I would meet up for dinner every Thursday evening at a restaurant near her college campus. Jake and I were still friendly toward one another and all of us, including Helen, would get together for the holidays, usually at the house, my house, because it was roomier. The house across the street sold quickly, as I knew it would, and a young couple with three young children and one on the way had moved in. I had only spoken to them a few times; however, Jolene knew them much better as she would babysit the kids occasionally when she was home for school breaks. Other than during the holidays or when Jolene would be home from school, I always felt lonely. Being in that big house all by myself since Teddy had passed away. I thought about getting another dog to keep me company, but I was still mourning the loss of Teddy...and I was still mourning the loss of Jeff.

For several months, I tried to find Jeff, well, whatever his name was, but had absolutely no luck. It was as if he just vanished. I still thought about him every single day and night. I missed him and I was still so in love with him, but I also knew for my own sake, I needed to eventually move on with my life and forget the past. I only wish I had never been able to remember. I still visit the ravine on occasion. It allows me to heal. Detective Bryant had concluded that night was just a tragic accident, one that would haunt me for the rest of my life.

I still have not fully regained my memory. I do not have explanations as to why I thought certain things occurred when they did not, yet I could not remember certain things that did occur. I still question moments in my life...were they real or part of a dream? My therapist said I may never remember everything. People say you do not dream while in a coma...but how does one really know?

After all this time, I still, occasionally, sit in front of the window and just stare across the street.

The End

ABOUT THE AUTHOR

Jeanna M. Marescalchi was born and raised in the city of Beverly, Massachusetts. She has two grown children, a daughter, Shannon and a son, Chad, both in their twenties. She and her husband, Keith, have been married for thirty years and they are proud grandparents to their granddaughter, Joella Mae, born in December of 2021. This is Jeanna's fourth published book but the first full story book she has written. Her other books include, "Me…Just Thinking!" "Me…Just Thinking, Again!" and "Me…Still Thinking!" all of which are collections of poetry, prose and short stories. She and her husband have moved to the Gulf Coast of Southern Florida where she hopes to continue writing books for her family, friends, and her readers to enjoy!